It had been an unus_____dn't descended to street le_____n lit up with large red lette_____ver the radio, "Emergency distress signal from a citizen with a wrist alarm."

Patrolman Jim Kelly hit the drop lever and started down. His partner, Tad Boleslaw, activated the night binocular screen. They found what they were looking for almost immediately.

"There they are," Boleslaw snapped. "Near the corner of Locust and MacArthur."

Suddenly there was a lance of flame between the two small figures below.

When they swept in, one of the figures was sprawled over the gutter. The other was standing, facing them. He held a gyro-jet rocket pistol in his right hand.

Boleslaw and Kelly vaulted out and drew their guns. "Drop it!" Kelly yelled.

"I'd rather not," the other replied with a grin.

"Drop that gun," Boleslaw said dangerously.

"Why don't you just try and take it from me?"

POLICE PATROL: 2000 A.D.

MACK REYNOLDS

ace books

A Division of Charter Communications Inc.
A GROSSET & DUNLAP COMPANY
1120 Avenue of the Americas
New York, New York 10036

POLICE PATROL: 2000 A.D.

Copyright © , 1977 by Mack Reynolds

Elements of this novel appeared in *Analog* under the titles, "Romp" and "Extortion, Inc." and in *Galaxy* under the titles, "Criminal in Utopia" and "Cry Wolf!"

An ACE Book

First Ace Printing: March, 1977

Printed in U.S.A.

I

Up until then, it had been an unusually uneventful night. They hadn't descended to street level even once. But now the screen lit up with large red letters and numbers, and a voice said urgently, "Emergency distress signal from citizen with wrist alarm."

Patrolman Jim Kelly hit the drop lever with the butt of his right hand and they started down. He flicked on speed. His partner beside him activated the night binocular screen.

Patrolman Tad Boleslaw knew the coordinates of their patrol area by heart. He snapped, "It's the corner of Locust and MacArthur. And, by holy Zoroaster, there they are!"

The police helio-jet came swooping in.

"On the ball, Tad," Kelly said, voice tense.

But Tad Boleslaw was already whipping his police .38 Recoilless from its quick-draw holster, his hand on the door next to him. They could make out two figures below in the otherwise deserted streets.

There couldn't have been two more divergent types. Jim Kelly was squat, husky, in his mid-forties; he was as ugly as an Irish monkey, easy and comfortable going. He was a long-time cop and didn't particularly mind the work but was still looking forward to retirement. Tad Boleslaw was in the vicinity of thirty, squarely handsome in the

Slavic tradition, blondish, wide of mouth, usually earnest of expression. He was big, but quick moving, and he didn't know it but the women who had loved him, in his time, were taken by the vulnerable quality in his blue eyes. He projected sincerity and dedication, and hadn't quite enough confidence in himself.

"Stick-up romp," Kelly growled.

The other patrolman didn't bother to answer that obvious statement.

Between the two small figures below there was suddenly a lance of flame.

"Holy Zoroaster, he nailed him," Boleslaw groaned. "Well, at least we'll get the funker."

When they swept in, one of the figures was sprawled over the gutter, half his body in the street, half on the sidewalk. Boleslaw vaulted out while they were still five or six feet off the ground and went charging up, .38 Recoilless in hand.

"Drop that gun!" he yelled.

The other was standing, facing Boleslaw, his hands at his sides and two feet or so out from his body. He had a gun in his right.

He said, "I'd rather not. It might damage it, hitting the sidewalk."

"Drop that gun," Boleslaw said dangerously. He had come to a halt and his own weapon was at the ready; his knees bent slightly, his left arm out for balance.

"Why not just take it from me?" the other said mildly. "You've got me covered and obviously nobody is so drivel-happy as to try to shoot it out with two trained police officers."

The patrolman scowled. This was a new one, he thought, and particularly since this character looked like a middle-aged clerk.

Kelly came running up, his own weapon in hand. He circled around, taking care not to get in the potential line of fire, came up behind the other man and grabbed the gun in question. He unnecessarily smelled the muzzle and then slipped it into a pocket of his tunic and gave the gunman a thorough frisking.

"Keep him covered," he told his partner, also unnecessarily, and went over and stared down at the body. There was a gaping hole in the fallen one's chest but the blood had already stopped pulsing. He was a youngster, probably in his late teens. Near his right hand was an old-fashioned revolver.

Jim Kelly turned back to the man Boleslaw was covering. He said, "Are you the one sent in the emergency alarm on the wrist gismo?"

"Yes."

"What happened?"

"Stick-up, I guess. I've never seen him before."

Tad Boleslaw said, "You must be awful quick on the draw if you took him when he already had you covered."

"Thanks. I guess he wasn't expecting me to be armed. When he heard your cruiser coming in, he looked up —kind of startled. That was long enough."

The two patrolmen sized him up. He was an unprepossessing man somewhere in his early fifties. He was a bit under average in size and could have used another ten pounds or so. He wore a mustache, and shouldn't have; he didn't have enough hair on his upper lip. He also wore

3

spectacles, which were rapidly becoming an anachronism in these days of eye surgery and the new model contact lenses.

Kelly thought inwardly, "No wonder the kid let him get the drop on him. He doesn't look as though he could kill time."

But then something else came to the veteran patrolman and he said, "Aren't you Buddy Brothers? Seems to me I've seen you down at the pistol range, working out with the fellows."

Brothers nodded. "I'm getting a little old to be called Buddy any more. The name's Charles Brothers. Yes, I'm kind of a junior member of the Police Pistol Team. I can't compete because I'm only a CAP. I'm a member of the City Auxiliary Police." He added, a touch of pride there, "It's too bad, because I can shoot circles around most of the boys."

Patrolman Boleslaw said in response to the incoming whine of sirens, "Here comes the meat wagon. This won't take long, Mr. Brothers. Then we'll run you down to headquarters and you can make a statement."

"Sure, boys. I've been through this before."

Tad Boleslaw eyed him in surprise and said, "You have?"

"Yes," Brothers said, looking around as though in explanation. "This is a pretty tough neighborhood."

"What in the hell are you doing here, this time of the night?"

"Walking home from work. I'm in Category Tabulating, Subdivision IBM. I'm on the swing shift. I don't get off until midnight."

Two vehicles, one an ambulance, came swooping

down. Uniformed officers, a plainclothesman and two white jacketed younger men with a stretcher spilled out.

The plainclothesman, obviously in charge, looked over the scene without change of expression. He had seen the scene before, though usually roles were reversed. Usually, it was the citizen stretched out on the street, the stick-up man caught, gun in hand, or shot down when he tried to resist or escape. Jim Kelly brought the confiscated gun from his tunic pocket and handed it over to the newcomer.

The plainclothesman was a little gone to weight, was tired of eyes and his hat, shoved back, indicated that he was beginning to bald. He smoked a well-charred, short pipe.

He said to Patrolman Boleslaw, "What happened, Tad?"

Boleslaw told him.

The plainclothesman turned to Brothers and said, "I'm Detective Lieutenant Norman Schmidt. You got a permit for this pistol you used on the punk?"

"Yes, sir."

The detective regarded him, and said, "You don't have to call me sir. You're a citizen and, I assume, a taxpayer. I work for the city."

The smaller man nodded. "I'm a member of the City Auxiliary Police, acting patrolman when on duty. I was helping you that time you led the squad against the Dolly Tetter gang sir."

Schmidt pretended to remember him now. "Oh, yeah," he said. "Well, good work, Brothers. Tad, you and Jim take him down to headquarters and make out a routine statement. Check his identity, so forth. Check out

5

his gun permit." He turned his eyes back to Charles Brothers. "No crud, but technically you're under arrest technically. You'll sleep in your own bed tonight."

"Thank you, sir," the little man said earnestly. "I suppose I'm a little upset. Uh, your men are certainly efficient. I have to congratulate you all. They were here in possibly half a minute after I activated my emergency distress alarm."

II

The next evening, before going onto his shift, Tad Boleslaw drifted into Lieutenant Schmidt's office. They were moderately good friends, considering rank differences. Tad's father and Schmidt had both been sergeants when the former had been killed in line of duty. The lieutenant knew that the younger man was bucking for the detective squad but didn't have the seniority as yet. Tad was third generation in the police category.

Schmidt had a marking stylo in his hand and was sourly checking out a report. He didn't like red tape and, Zoroaster knew, there was enough of it these days.

He said, "Cheers, Tad. What spins with you?" He ran a freckled hand over his less than generously haired head wearily.

Tad pulled up one of the steel chairs of the drab police office without invitation.

He said, scowling a little, "I was wondering about that gunning last night."

The older man tossed his stylo to the desk, glad of the opportunity to scuttle it, and reached for his well-soured pipe. "What gunning? There were three. Center City is getting to be like a shooting gallery. Oh, you mean the one you and Jim Kelly were in on. What about it?"

7

"I don't know. It was something Brothers said. He said it wasn't the first time he'd gone through this. He doesn't exactly look the Wyatt Earp, Wild Bill Hickok type. But last night he evidently drew on that young funker while the kid was leveled down on him."

Schmidt laughed, even as he loaded the briar. "This Charles Brothers I checked out, just in routine. In spite of his looks, he's an Asian-war hero. Bronze Star. He's seen a gun or so before, in his time."

Tad said, "All right, but in the name of holy Zoroaster what's he doing living in that neighborhood? And, if he does, what in the hell's he doing walking back and forth to work at night? Why doesn't he drive or at least take public transportation? We've got a pretty good vacuum-transport metro in Center City these days. He could get to within a block of his house on it."

The lieutenant contemplated him, even as he lit his pipe. "What are you getting at, Tad?"

"He said he'd been through it before. How many times?"

Schmidt said, "Like I say, I checked him out just as routine. He's one of the first citizens in Center City to buy an emergency wrist device. And he was one of the first to use it. Two guys jumped him and he had it out with them. By the time the patrol boys got there, he had finished them off. We were looking for both of them, since they both had nice long records on their crime dossiers. One had a gun we were also looking for since a slug from it had chilled one of the citizens over in Far Cry. The other's gun wasn't hot, so far as we know."

Tad said, "That was the first time. You mean that there were more?"

8

"The next time, the man who tried to mug him didn't have a crime dossier. Nothing at all. Brothers nailed him before the funker got off a single shot. That gyro-jet rocket pistol he packs needs exactly one hit to demolish King Kong or Moby Dick."

"How was the mugger armed?"

The lieutenant said, "With one of these bureau drawer specials left over from the old days when you could buy these foreign-made war-surplus shooters for about fifteen dollars apiece. No record of the serial number, of course."

Tad frowned and said, "Aren't they getting kind of scarce these days?"

"What are you building up to?"

"Damned if I know. How did that gun the kid had last night check out?"

"Same thing. You can still pick them up in that slob neighborhood for the equivalent of a few pseudo-dollars. What they do is trade them around to avoid any record in the data banks. What in the hell's roaching you, Tad?" The lieutenant had gotten his pipe going well. It stank.

The patrolman said unhappily, "Walking home at night, in that neighborhood. It looks like he's asking for it. His luck can't last forever."

Schmidt shrugged lardy shoulders. "The guy's got guts. He's not afraid of these punks. If more citizens were like him, had his courage, the muggers wouldn't be on the streets. I told you, he's even got medals. You think a bunch of young funkers looking for something to flog to buy their next fix of trank or soma are going to scare him off the streets of the city?"

Tad said sourly, "They're either going to or he's going

9

to wind up in the gutter himself one of these nights. He's had more shootouts than most of the patrolmen on the force."

He came to his feet, preparatory to leaving but the lieutenant pulled out a drawer, reached in and came up with a gyro-jet rocket pistol.

Schmidt said, "This is Brothers' gun. All charges have been dropped against him, of course. When you and Jim Kelly get over to that neighborhood, take it back to him."

Tad Boleslaw took the weapon and looked at it distastefully. "I don't like these things," he said. "Too much gun. You hit a man, just anywhere at all, and if he doesn't go down you walk around behind him to see what's holding him up. Suppose somebody's running and you want to shoot him in the leg to stop him. You shoot him with one of these and it'd blow his leg off and he'd probably bleed to death before you could get medical help."

"Yeah," Schmidt said around his pipe stem, "but you're a cop and sometimes the occasion comes up when you want to shoot some funker who's running in the leg. But Charles Brothers carries his shooter for self-defense and when you're defending your life the more punch you have on hand the better."

"I suppose so," Tad said, still not happy. "See you later, Norm."

III

Since Charles Brothers had told them he worked the swing shift, Tad and Jim Kelly put off going to his home until about one in the morning. Even knowing the neighborhood, both of the patrolmen were surprised at the squalid, aged apartment house that the man lived in.

The whole ward was a blot on the city and periodically the city fathers drew up plans to renovate it. Nothing seemed to come of the plans. Popularly, it was known as the last of the slums and the residents were aliens and others not eligible to collect the federal dividends from Inalienable Basic which was sufficient to enable the unemployed or pensioners to rent a small apartment in a decent high-rise apartment house, or even a place out in the suburbs. You didn't live very high on the hog on Inalienable Basic but you lived adequately. One of the reasons for the high crime rate in this neighborhood was because so many of the residents were felons on the lam, military deserters, or others afraid to register for Inalienable Basic because they couldn't reveal their correct identity.

But it was unlikely that Charles Brothers would live here.

They parked their helio-jet patrol vehicle in front of the

11

building and both of them got out. They looked at the aged structure; it must have been well over a century old.

"Some joint," Jim said. "Let's go. I hate to leave our heap here. In this vicinity, somebody might steal it."

They went up the stone steps to the door. There was no identity screen. Instead, there were eight names and eight old-fashioned electric buttons there. One of the name plates read Charles and Tilly Brothers. Apartment Six. Tad pressed the appropriate button and shortly the door buzzed. Jim opened it and they went on into a dimly lit hall. There was no elevator. They started up the stairs.

Apartment Six was on the third floor. Evidently, there were two flats per floor. Jim knocked on the door.

There was a peephole set into it and the two patrolmen could detect an eye taking them in. The door opened and Charles Brothers was there in shirtsleeves, pants and slippers.

He said, "Yes? What can I do for you?"

Tad said, "The lieutenant sent us over to return your gun, Mr. Brothers. All charges against you have been dropped."

"Why, come on in, boys."

They followed him into a living room. In actuality, once inside the apartment it wasn't badly done at all. It was very well, very tastefully, furnished and there were paintings on the walls that were obviously originals.

A girl got up from the couch on which she had been seated and, of all things, knitting. Who ever heard of women knitting any more in this age of mass produced ultra-textiles? She looked at the two police officers nervously.

She wasn't an unattractive young woman. About

12

twenty-five, Tad would say. Nice brown hair worn rather long as styles went these days, pleasant figure just a very little on the dumpy side, and, like Charles Brothers himself, she wore glasses. If anything, they enhanced her blue eyes. Her clothes were a good twenty years out of date.

Brothers said, "Gentlemen, this is my daughter, Tilly. Tilly, these are the two officers who came to my rescue last night." He added, apologetically, "I don't believe that I got your names."

Tad grinned at her, his cap already in hand, and said, "He didn't need to be rescued. I'm patrolman Tadeusz Boleslaw and this is Patrolman James Kelly."

Brothers looked at him and said, "Are you a foreigner?"

Tad frowned and said, "Why, no. My father was of Polish descent and my mother German, but they were both second generation Americans. Why?"

Brothers said uncomfortably, "I don't like foreigners. I'd offer you boys a drink but I no longer use the stuff myself. It cuts down your reflexes. For that matter, I don't hold with keeping it in the house."

Kelly said, "We're not allowed to drink on duty anyway."

And Tilly said, in a small, distinct, sweet voice, "Coffee, perhaps? Won't you gentlemen be seated?"

Tad smiled at her. "Afraid we don't have time, Ms. Brothers. We'll take a rain check." He looked at her father, preparatory to leaving. He had already handed over the deadly gyro-jet rocket pistol. He said, "Hope you don't have to use that again, sir."

"I trust I won't but I like to be prepared," Brothers told him. "These gook slum elements have to be kept down."

Jim said, "I hope you didn't walk home tonight through this neighborhood."

"Why, yes, of course I did," Brothers said, a touch of indignation in his voice. "I do every night. I have a sedentary job and need the exercise."

"Unarmed?"

The small man shook his head, as though smug. "No. I had another gun. I collect guns."

Tad nodded, as though that figured, and said, "Well, goodnight. Nice to have met you, Ms. Brothers."

On the way down the steps, Tad muttered, "That's a funny set-up there."

Kelly looked at him from the side of his eyes. "How do you mean?"

"I don't know."

Back on their patrol over the city, Tad said, "Did you notice that the girl wore an emergency wrist alarm too?"

"Why not? I wish the hell every citizen did," Jim told him. "Biggest thing to hinder crime we've ever had. The Federal Enforcement Assistance Administration came up with the first primitive one way back in the 1970s. But they're really efficient now. A citizen is confronted with an emergency and activates his wrist alarm. The computers, within less than a second, get a cross on his location and beam a message to the nearest patrol vehicles, both surface and air. Wizard! We're on the scene, often in less than a minute, like last night. How can you beat it? Burglaries, for instance. Except for burglaries of empty houses, they've just about disappeared. And rape? Any girl with a wrist alarm is as safe as in her mother's arms."

"I guess you're right," Tad said. "Everybody ought to wear one, especially if they're open to violence."

Jim was suddenly scowling. "You know," he said, "it just came to me, talking about wrist emergency alarms. Brothers wasn't wearing one last night."

"What're you talking about?" Tad said, puzzled. "How could he have sent in that emergency call, if he didn't have an alarm?"

"I'm not saying he didn't have one. I'm just saying he wasn't wearing one on his wrist. Remember when I frisked him? I ran my hands up his forearms. I always do, to check for knives or little hide-out pistols. He wasn't wearing anything on his wrists, not even a chronometer."

"He probably had it in his pocket," Tad said. "You wouldn't have reacted to something like that in a pocket."

"Why? They make those alarms as big as they are so that potential stick-up men or muggers, or whatever, can see them and be scared off. There's not much point in hiding your wrist alarm."

They flew in silence for a time until Tad said, "What got me there was the uncomfortable atmosphere. The girl acted as though she was afraid. When we first came in, she was upset."

Jim looked at him quizzically. "Afraid of what? Not a couple of cops. Hell, her father's a cop himself, in a way. Volunteer in the City Auxiliary Police. From what he told Norm Schmidt, he evidently was in that shoot-out with Dolly Tetter's mob."

"I don't mean immediately afraid," Tad said slowly. "I mean a long time afraid. There was a certain feeling of fear in that apartment."

"Holy jumping Zoroaster," Jim said in disgust. "You going mystical on me? Next thing you'll be reading tea leaves."

15

IV

Rex Moran flicked the stud on his transeiver to give him the time and looked at the clock face that appeared on the screen. A robot computer voice said, ''When the bell rings it will be exactly two minutes until eight hours.'' A tiny bell rang.

Rex Moran grunted and looked about the small, drab apartment. He had better get going.

First, though, he took his Universal Credit Card from an inner pocket of his jacket and inserted it in the slot of his standard phone screen which sat on his living-cum-bedroom's sole table. He said into the screen, ''Credit balance check, please.''

Within seconds, a robot voice said, ''Ten shares of Inalienable Basic. No shares of Variable Basic. Current cash credit, one pseudo-dollar and twenty-three cents.''

''One pseudo-dollar and twenty-three cents,'' he muttered, though grinning. ''Holy living Zoroaster, I didn't think I'd have to start with that little on hand.''

He dialed Credit and waited until a face faded in on the screen. It was a businesslike, brisk, possibly impatient, face.

It said, ''Jason May, here. Assistant Credit Manager, Inalienable Basic Dividends.''

Rex Moran put his Uni-Credit Card on the screen and said, ''I'd like an advance on my dividends.''

May was seated at a desk. "Just a moment, please," he said, and evidently pressed a button. He listened to a report on a desk phone screen and then looked back at Moran. "According to the records, you're already two months ahead."

"I know that," Rex said doggedly, "but it's an emergency."

"It is always an emergency, Mr. Moran," May said flatly. "What is the emergency? The records show that you are almost invariably as far ahead as you can get on your monthly dividends. As you must know, the government charges interest on such advances. In the long run, you lose, Mr. Moran."

"I know, I know," Rex Moran said, an element of complaint in his voice. "I've had a long spell of bad luck. One thing after another."

"I would suggest you adjust your way of living to your income, which would seem to consist of nothimg except your Inalienable Basic stock dividends. It has been increasing year after year and should be sufficient for a modest way of life. What is the current emergency, please?"

Rex Moran wished he had thought this out in more detail before launching into his fling. He said, "I've got a sick brother I have to help."

"Where is this brother, Mr. Moran?"

"In Panama City."

"One moment, please." May went back to one of his desk screens. In only moments, he looked up again with a sigh. "Mr. Moran, the computer banks have no records of you having a brother at all, in Panama City or anywhere else. Request denied. And, Mr. Moran . . ."

"Yeah?" Rex Moran said in disgust.

17

"It is a minor offense to lie to a credit manager in attempt to secure an advance on dividends. I shall take no action on this occasion, but the fact will be entered on your record in the National Data Banks."

"Oh, great," Rex Moran growled. He flicked off his screen. "I didn't expect that to work anyway," he muttered.

He thought over his plans for a few minutes, then squared his shoulders and dialed the local branch of the ultra-market on his auto-delivery box. He was a man in his early thirties, mildly burly in build and with a not really unpleasant face in spite of the broken nose of one who has either seen military combat, or perhaps been a pugilist. In reality, neither was the case.

The ultra-market in the screen, he dialed the children's toy section, boy's toys and then military-type toys. He narrowed it down to guns and dialed one that came to only seventy-cents. It would have to do. He put his Uni-Credit Card in the slot, his thumbprint on the screen and ordered the toy.

Within moments, it was in the vacuum delivery box, and he put it in the side pocket of his jacket. It was on the smallish side, but black and at any distance at all looked realistic enough for his purpose.

He moved over to his library booster screen and dialed a newspaper, then the paper of two weeks previous, and the obituaries.

He went through several papers before he found the one that seemed most likely, by the address and the information in the item, and made some notes with his stylo.

Finally, he dialed the address and waited until a face faded in on his phone screen.

The face frowned at him in lack of recognition.

Rex Moran said, "Mr. Vassilis? My name is Roy McCord."

Vassilis was a tired looking obvious aristocrat, perhaps a few years on the other side of sixty.

Still frowning, he said, "What can I do for you, Mr. McCord?"

"I just got back into town and heard the news about —well, the bad news. I'm a friend—forgive me, Mr. Vassilis—*was* a friend of Jerry—Jerome."

The man's face lightened a bit and then went sad. He said, "Ah, I see. I am afraid he hadn't mentioned your name, but then, Jerome had many friends of whom I knew little."

"Yes, sir. I'd like the opportunity to offer my condolences in person," Rex Moran began.

The older man was frowning slightly and began to respond.

But Moran hurried on. "But I also have something of Jerry's that I suppose should go to you, sir."

"Something of Jerome's. But what?"

Rex Moran managed to look slightly embarrassed. "Well, sir, I—well, I think it would be better if I just brought it over."

The older man was mystified. However, he shrugged thin shoulders. "Very well, young man. Let me see, I shall be free at, say, nine hours this morning and should be able to give you a few minutes."

"Fine, sir. I'll be there." Rex Moran switched off the screen before the other could say anything further.

For a moment he stared down at the blank screen, then shifted muscles in his shoulders. "First step," he said aloud. "So far, so good. Maybe I shouldn't have used this phone, but in the long run it won't make any difference."

He didn't take the vacuum-tube metro from his own building, knowing that a record was kept of all trips in the computer banks and the john-fuzz might trace back later on his Uni-Credit Card number. Instead, he walked several blocks and entered a public metro terminal.

He looked up at the map and selected another terminal a couple of blocks from his destination, then entered the next twenty-seater going through that point. After putting his credit card in the payment slot, he realized that with the buying of the toy gun, he probably had only a few cents left to his balance in the National Data Banks. He didn't even have enough credit left to get back to his apartment if this little romp pickled. What a laugh that would give the boys if he had to walk home.

He left the vacuum-tube transport terminal and walked to the building where Vassilis lived. This was the crucial point now. If there were others present, his plan had come a cropper. However, if he had read between the lines correctly, the senior Mr. Vassilis lived alone in his apartment in this swank neighborhood. The obituary had said he was the sole survivor.

There was an identity screen on the front entry. Keeping his fingers crossed that his Universal Credit Card wouldn't be required for entrance identification, he said into the screen, "Roy McCord, on appointment to see Mr. Frank Vassilis."

The door opened and he stepped through.

The Vassilis apartment was on the next to top floor. Rex Moran got out of the elevator, found a door with the Vassilis name on it and activated the door screen. When it lit up, he said into it, "Roy McCord, calling on Mr. Vassilis by appointment."

The door opened and he entered.

And came to a halt. The man standing there in a dark suit was not the Mr. Vassilis he had spoken to earlier on the phone screen. This worthy was a stiffish type of possibly fifty. His eyes went up and down Rex Moran superciliously, taking in the less-than-elegant suit, taking in the rugged features.

He said, "Yes, sir. Mr. McCord? The master is await- ing you in his escape sanctum."

The *master?* Holy jumping Zoroaster, Vassilis had a man servant. Whoever heard of personal servants in this day and age? The obituary had hinted that the old boy was upper-class, but Rex Moran hadn't been thinking in terms of something so rich as an establishment with a servant.

However, he followed along. It was the largest apart- ment he could, offhand, ever remember having been in. They went down one hall, turned to the right and then down another one.

There was no identity screen on the door they stopped in front of. The servant knocked gently and opened the door before there was any reply. Evidently, old Vassilis was expecting him, all right.

The servant stood stiffly and said, "Mr. McCord, sir."

The elderly man Rex Moran had talked to on the phone screen earlier looked up from where he sat in a comfort chair, a small magnifying glass in one hand, a dozen or more stamps on a small table before him. He was evi- dently a philatelist.

He said, "Ah, yes. Mr. Roy McCord, Jerome's friend. Please come in." As the servant had before him, he took in Moran's clothing and general appearance and his eyebrows went up. Obviously, Moran didn't seem the type that his deceased son would have associated with.

But he said, "Now what is it I can do for you, Mr. McCord? You mentioned something of Jerome's."

Rex Moran looked at the servant.

Vassilis said, "That will be all, Franklin."

The servant said, "Yes, sir," and turned and left, closing the door quietly behind him.

No need to mince around. Rex Moran brought the toy gun from his pocket briefly, let Vassilis glimpse it, and returned it to his side pocket, but still held it in his hand.

He said, "This is a romp, Mr. Vassilis."

The other goggled at him. "You—you mean that you are a thief? That you got into my home under false pretenses? Why, you didn't know Jerome at all!"

Moran let his face go empty. He said, "I wouldn't put it that way. Let's just say that I'm tired of not getting my share of the cake. And since the powers that be won't give it to me, I'm taking it."

The old man stared at him in disgust. "You are a fool, young man."

"Maybe, maybe not." Rex Moran jiggled the gun in his side pocket, suggestively.

The older man said, "Being a thief simply doesn't make sense in this day. Society has made arrangements to defend itself against the thief. There's not enough profit in petty crime to pay off."

Rex Moran grinned at him sourly and said, "Perhaps I didn't exactly have petty crime in mind, Mr. Vassilis. Now, hand me your Universal Credit Card."

The old man was taken aback. He said, "What other kind of crime is possible? Nobody but I can spend my pseudo-dollars. I can't give them away, gamble them away, throw them away, or be cheated out of them. Only I can spend my dividends.''

''We'll see about that,'' Rex Moran nodded. ''Now, let's have your Universal Credit Card.'' He jiggled the gun in his pocket again.

The older man contemptuously took a beautiful leather wallet from an inner pocket and brought forth a standard Uni-Credit Card. He handed it over.

Moran said, ''You have a vacuum delivery box in this room? Oh, yeah, here we are. Zoroaster, look at the size of it. Now that's the advantage of being an upper-class like you, Mr. Vassilis. You should see the teeny auto-delivery box in my mini-apartment. If I want anything of any size at all, I've got to use the box down in the lobby of the crummy building I'm in. Now, with a nice big vacuum delivery box like this anything you wanted would have to be really super-size before you couldn't get it delivered right here in your escape sanctum.''

Vassilis said, ''You are a fool, young man. The officials will be after you in no time flat.''

Moran grinned at him again and sat down before the box, keeping an eye on him. He put the card in the phone screen's slot and said, ''Credit balance, please.''

A computer robot voice said, ''Ten shares of Inalienable Basic. Two thousand and forty-six shares of Variable Basic. Current cash credit, forty-two thousand and twenty-nine pseudo-dollars and eighteen cents.''

Rex Moran whistled. ''Two thousand-and-forty-six-shares-of-Variable. Zoroaster!''

Vassilis grunted contempt of him.

Moran dialed the ultra-market, then sports, then finally, arms, then handguns. He selected a .38 Magnum Auto-

matic and dialed it and a box of cartridges. He thought for
a moment, then dialed photography and selected a Poloroid-Pentax and some film for it.

"Might as well do this up brown," he said conversa-
tionally to the older man. "Might as well put a *generous*
hole in that credit balance."

"There'll be no hole—as you call it—at all," Vassilis
said bitterly. "When I report this thievery, the authorities
will return to my account the sum involved in any depre-
ciations you have performed."

Rex Moran dialed men's clothing and took his time in
selecting a full outfit, including shoes.

"Now this is the crucial point," he said thoughtfully, to
no one in particular. He dialed jewelry and finally selected
a two thousand pseudo-dollar blue diamond ring.

"I guess that's it," he said. Then, "Oh, one other
thing." He dialed sports again, and camping, and eventually a length of rope.

He turned back to Frank Vassilis and said, "And now,
old man, come on over here and stick your thumbprint on
this order screen."

"Suppose I refuse?"

Rex Moran grinned at him. "Why should you? Like
you said, when you report this, the authorities will return
your pseudo-dollar credit to you and come looking for me.
You're not losing anything."

The older man, grumbling, came erect in his chair,
stood and walked over to the vacuum delivery box and,
with a sneer of contempt for his intruder, stuck his right
thumb print on the screen.

Moments later, the articles had arrived. Vassilis returned to his comfort chair.

Rex Moran began fishing the articles he had ordered

from the box. He loaded the gun, put it next to him within handy reach and then stripped and dressed in his new clothes.

There was a bathroom connecting with the escape sanctum. Keeping a wary eye on the old man, he carried his old clothes and shoes over to it, opened the door, and without leaving Vassilis's presence, tossed them all into the disposal chute there.

"Wouldn't do to leave the john-fuzz any clues," he said cheerfully.

He took the camera and slung it over his shoulder. He looked at the ring admiringly and tucked it away in an inner pocket and then the gun and the box of bullets.

He pulled the Universal Credit Card from the slot and tucked it away as well.

"What in the world do you want that for?" his victim protested. "I'll just have to go through the trouble of getting another one issued to me."

"I'll never tell," Moran grinned.

Still looking at the ring, he muttered, "I have half a mind to order a few more of these but that's a big drain on your account all at the same time and it might throw some relays and have the computer people check here."

"Thief," Vassilis said bitterly.

Moran grinned at him still once again. "What's your beef? It won't be you who loses."

He took up the rope. "First we'll tie you up a bit, old chum-pal, and then we'll call in Franklin, or whatever his name is, and do a job on him. It wouldn't do for you to call the john-fuzz, before I even get out of the building."

"You'll never get away with this, you young cloddy," the old man bit out.

"Famous last words," Moran grinned back at him.

25

V

Tad Boleslaw and Jim Kelly were patrolling a different city area than their usual sector and were on a day shift, rather than night, when the call came in. They were taking over for a team of fellow helio-jet policemen who were on vacation.

The screen lit up and there was more than the usual urgency in the voice of the sergeant on duty at the headquarters station.

He snapped, "Armed robbery. Berkeley Apartments. Apartment 90B."

Jim Kelly, who was at the controls, was already throwing on power and deftly spinning the police helio-jet patrol vehicle to the new direction.

Tad said to the sergeant, "Are there any details, Sam? What's it all about?"

"The victim is Frank Vassilis. Just a moment, dope is coming in on him from the data banks. Sixty-four years of age. Widower. Retired mining engineer. Lives alone. Evidently, quite a big mucky-muck in his day."

"Must be, to have been able to get a pad in the Berkeley," Kelly muttered. "Hell, they're the poshiest residential apartments in town."

They swooped down in front of the high-rise and were dashing for the door almost before their vehicle came to a halt. They darted across the lavish lobby and into an elevator whose door was just beginning to close. There were two somewhat startled looking occupants, a middle-aged couple.

Tad said quickly, "Police. Emergency. Please take another elevator."

The man began to protest. "I say. . . . "

But his wife was already hurrying out of the compartment, looking back over her shoulder, wide-eyed. On the face of it, police officers were a rarity in the Berkeley. Her husband followed her, huffily.

Jim Kelly said into the screen, "Apartment 90B, immediately. No stops. This is a police matter."

"Yes, officer," the metallic computer voice said, and they took off.

They bent their knees to accommodate to the acceleration. The ninetieth floor got express service.

At that lofty height, they hurried out as soon as the elevator door was open enough to allow exit. Both dragged their guns from their holsters.

There were signs on the wall opposite. Only six of them. It would seem that there were but that number of suites on the whole floor. Swank indeed.

"This way," Tad got out, needlessly. They hurried down the corridor and found apartment 90B without any difficulty.

They stood before the identity screen, but Jim Kelly also banged impatiently with the barrel of his .38 Recoilless. The door opened and they hurried in, guns at the ready.

They were greeted by an aloof-looking character in his middle years.

Before he remembered that headquarters had told them

that the robbery victim was in his mid-sixties, Tad blurted, "Mr. Vassilis?"

Vassilis took in the drawn weapons and lifted his nostrils. He said, "The affair took place over half an hour ago. The miscreant has long since departed. No. I am Franklin. Mr. Vassilis is in his escape sanctum."

Tad and Jim put away their guns, somewhat as though abashed, and followed.

The escape sanctum was the most well-done study Tad had ever seen. There were endless shelves of old-fashioned, hard cover books, in a day when most people did their reading on a library booster screen from the National Data Banks. There were a dozen or so paintings, ranging back to the Impressionists. There were two mounted hunting trophies, both of them large cats; one was a tiger, the other something else that Tad didn't recognize but which was jet black. There were five guns in a wooden rack, three rifles and two shotguns. The furniture looked as though it was meant for comfort rather than show. The kind of comfort where you stretched out with your shoes on, on the extra-large leather couch.

At the desk, an old timer was fiddling around with what looked like postage stamps. Postage stamps hadn't been in use since Tad was a boy.

Tad said, "Mr. Vassilis?"

The old timer looked up. He said, "It took you long enough to get here. I had heard that you chaps were supposed to be ultra-efficient these days."

Jim Kelly said, "It took us less than two minutes to get to the Berkeley Apartments after receiving the signal. The rest of the time was spent getting up this far—the ninetieth floor."

The old man put down his stamp tweezer and magnifying glass. He said, "Very well, this is the first time I have been robbed since I was a young man, and the first time I have ever been robbed in the United States of the Americas. What is the procedure?"

Tad brought a notebook from his jacket pocket and a stylo. Jim Kelly brought forth his transeiver, activated it and dialed it for police records.

Vassilis said, "Sit down, gentlemen."

They found chairs.

Tad said, "Can you give us the story as quickly as possible, sir? He might still be in the vicinity."

"I doubt it," the old man said. "He seemed surprisingly capable." He scowled. "Especially in view of the fact that the, ah, romp, I believe is the term, was so ridiculous."

"Let's have his description," Tad said.

The old boy gave them a surprisingly good rundown on the appearance of the robber.

Jim said, "Well, if he looked like such a bum, and dressed like one, how in the hell . . . that is, how did he ever get into a place like this?"

Vassilis said unhappily, "My son died recently. He phoned saying he was Roy McCord and he claimed to be a friend of Jerome—he called him Jerry—and said he had something of Jerome's that he thought I should have. As a result, I cleared him through to my apartment, on the elevator computers and so forth."

"An old wheeze," Tad said, "but one that you don't run into much any more. Not much purpose. He probably went through the newspapers, picked up your son's obituary, saw that you lived in an expensive building, and went into his pitch."

"I had already come to that conclusion," the old man

said testily. "One is not as sharp-witted as one might be under such circumstances. Jerome's untimely death still weighs heavily on me."

"Yes, sir," Tad said respectfully. "Sorry. What did he steal?"

"My Universal Credit Card."

The two policemen stared at him.

Jim blurted, "What in the hell good . . . uh, that is, why would he steal your Uni-Credit Card? What good would it do him? Nobody can use it but you."

"How would I know? First he utilized it to purchase clothes, a gun and ammunition, an expensive camera and a two thousand pseudo-dollar diamond ring."

They were both still looking at him as though what he had said was idiotic.

"A gun?" Tad said finally. "I undersood that he had stuck you up. He must have already had a gun. He'd be drivel-happy to get another one on your Uni-Credit Card. It's a registered number and everything is now recorded in the National Data Banks. Every time it goes off will be automatically recorded in the data banks and they'll have a fix on it, and him." Tad looked at his partner. "Jim, get on the screen. Get the model and registration of that gun. It was ordered on Mr. Vassilis' credit card. Put out an alarm for an immediate fix on it, if it's used."

"Yeah, sure," Jim said and went over to the screen on the old man's desk and began doing the necessary.

Tad said, "He took your credit card with him?"

"I already told you that."

"Yes, but I can't figure out why. Do you remember the number? It's not important. We can check it through the data banks."

"Of course, I remember my credit card number. I'm not quite senile yet, you know. It's A-3-5478-W-29. So far as his ordering a second gun is concerned, I now suspect that the first one wasn't authentic. He let me get only the barest glimpse of it before putting it into his jacket pocket."

Jim Kelly had finished at the phone screen and returned. He said, unbelievingly, "And he was just able to dial a handgun. . . ."

"And ammunition," the oldster put in.

"Just like that? No getting a permit, or anything? It's not as easy as that to buy a handgun these days."

Vassilis looked at him in scorn. "I have been cleared for buying firearms for more than fifty years, young man. The purchase was made with my identification."

Tad said, "And he forced you to put your thumbprint on the credit screen?"

"Certainly. I am not such a dolt as to resist a muscular young man with a gun. Particularly in view of the fact that I have actually lost nothing. All of my pseudo-dollar credits will be returned to me."

Kelly shook his head. "This is the silliest romp I've ever heard of. Did he act as though he was on something?"

"On something?"

"Some kind of dope. Soma, trank, or whatever. Or was he drunk?"

"Not so far as I know," the old man said. "In my travels I have seen a good many chaps under the influence of various narcotics, not to speak of seeing a good many drunks. He was alert, seemingly quite intelligent, seemingly with a moderately good education. And the pupils of his eyes were not dilated, as would have particularly applied if he had recent taken any of the opium derivities."

Tad said, "How do you mean he seemed to have a moderately good education?"

Vassilis was impatient. "In my time, it was necessary for me to be able to judge men. His voice was that of a man who has spent at least some time in a university."

Jim Kelly said, "Can you describe these new clothes that he bought with your Uni-Credit Card? I don't imagine that considering the stress you were under . . . "

The retired engineer both could and did describe the clothing, in considerable detail.

Tad said, "All right, after he ordered all these things, what happened?"

"He ordered some rope and tied me up, and then my man, Franklin, here."

Kelly said, "How'd you get loose?"

The old man looked at him. "I have been tied up before in my time."

He was quite an old duffer, Tad decided. But they were getting nowhere. Something came to him.

"This diamond ring he bought. Was it a man's ring or woman's?"

"Why, I believe it was a woman's."

Tad looked at his sidekick, then back at the victim. "Would you say he was the type who'd steal a ring for his girl friend?"

Vassilis shook his head. "As I told you, when he first appeared, he was on the seedy side. I would think other more immediate and relevant matters would be on his mind."

Tad said to Jim, "Let's go. I think that possibly I might have something." He looked back to Vassilis. "We'll keep you informed, sir."

The old man took up his magnifying glass. "It's not of a great deal of importance to me," he said gruffly. "As I've said, in the long run I will have lost nothing. It's simply that I don't like to have a gun pointed at me in my own home."

Franklin showed the two patrolmen to the door.

Back on the street, after leaving the building that housed Frank Vassilis' establishment, Rex Moran had realized that it was going to be necessary for him to walk to his next destination. His credit standing simply did not allow even such a small sum as riding in the vacuum tubes. However, happily, it wasn't as far as all that. As he walked, he took the toy gun from his pocket and threw it into a waste receptacle. He had the real thing now.

He found the neighborhood and had a choice of three alternatives. He took the smallest of the shops and entered.

There were even a few display cases. How anachronistic could you get? He grunted sour amusement to himself; here was the last of the kulaks, the last of the small businessmen.

A quiet man of about fifty entered from a back room and took Rex Moran in before saying in a soft voice, "Yes, sir, what can I do for you?" Obviously, the potential customer's excellent clothes had impressed themselves upon him.

Rex Moran went into his act. Hesitantly, he said, "I understand that you sometimes buy personal property."

"That is correct. Buy and sell. Sometimes on consignment. But what type of property, Mr. . . ?"

"Adams," Rex Moran said. "Timothy Adams. I have a ring that used to belong to my mother. It is of no value to me now, and I thought—well I might as well realize what pseudo-dollar credit value it has."

"I see. Please sit down, Mr. Adams. Heirloom jewelry is a bit of a drug on the market, but we can take a look." He sat himself behind a desk and motioned to a straight chair.

Rex Moran sat down and brought the diamond ring from his pocket and proffered it. The other took it and set it on the table.

He looked at Rex Moran thoughtfully. "This is a very modern setting, Mr. Adams. I had gained that impression that it was an older piece your mother had left you."

"Oh, no," Rex Moran said. "She bought it not too very long before she died. If I had a wife or someone, I might give it to her, but I haven't."

The man looked at him. He said, "Mr. Adams, I am not a fence, you know. This is a legitimate business."

"Fence?" Rex Moran said blankly.

"I buy and sell such items as art objects and jewelry, but I do not receive stolen goods. Where did you say your mother bought this?"

"On a vacation in Common Europe. In Paris, I think, or possibly Rome."

"So it would be untraceable here in the United States of the Americas."

"Why, it never occurred to me. Who in the world would want to trace it?"

The shop owner took up the ring and looked at it

34

thoughtfully. He brought a jeweler's glass from a drawer and peered through it.

He put the ring down finally and looked at Rex Moran. "I'll give you two hundred pseudo-dollars for it."

"Two hundred pseudo-dollars! My mother said that she had paid more than two thousand pseudo-dollars for it."

"Then she paid too much. The mark-up on jewelry is very high, Mr. Adams, and such items as this can take a long time to move. I might have to hold it here in the shop for months, or even years."

Rex Moran thought about it, his expression hesitant. He said finally, "Make it three hundred."

The other considered that. "Very well," he said. "But I'm making a mistake."

"Yeah," Rex Moran said sourly. He brought his Universal Credit Card from his pocket and stuck it into one of the slots on the proprietor's exchange screen.

The shop owner put the ring in a drawer, brought forth his own Universal Credit Card and put it into the other exchange slot. Both of them put their thumbprints on the identity square of the screen. The owner of the shop said, "Please transfer the amount of three hundred pseudo-dollars from my account to this other card."

A robot computer voice said, "Transfer completed."

Rex Moran retrieved his credit card and returned it to his pocket even as he came to his feet. "I still think I was robbed," he muttered.

The other said nothing, simply sat there and watched after him as Rex Moran left the shop. When he was gone the shop owner opened the drawer and took out the diamond ring and looked at it in satisfaction.

VI

Back in the helio-jet patrol vehicle, Jim Kelly looked skeptically at his partner. He said, "What in the hell do you have in mind? This is one of the silliest things I've ever run into. What in the hell's he going to do with the old boy's Uni-Credit Card? He can't use it without Vassilis' thumbprint to finalize the transaction. And we've already got the card's number alerted in the computer banks. The moment he even tries to use it, they'll get a fix on him and we'll land on him like a ton of manure. We should have asked Vassilis if the guy looked like a psycho."

"Not from what he said," Tad told him. "Now look, he ordered a two thousand pseudo-dollar diamond ring. A woman's ring. In short, he didn't plan to wear it himself and from what the old boy said, he was in no shape to be picking up do-dads for his girl friend. His immediate problem is to raise funds."

"What are you driving at?"

"Get on the National Data Banks and locate the nearest shops in this vicinity that buy antiques, used jewelry heirlooms, that sort of thing. I'm guessing that he's going to try and flog that diamond ring as quickly as possible, before we send out an alert on it. He thinks that he's got a little time. It would ordinarily take us at least a few hours to check the ultra-market and get a really accurate description and photograph of it."

36

Jim looked at him. "Why two thousand? Why didn't he order a five thousand pseudo-dollar ring?" But Jim Kelly was already dialing the data banks.

Ted said thoughtfully, "It's about the highest amount you could fence without getting too much attention. Maybe he could have ordered several two thousand ones and flogged them at different places."

"Why didn't he?"

"I don't know. Possibly he was afraid of alerting the ultra-market if he was too greedy."

Jim shook his head. "It still sounds like the silliest romp I ever ran into, pulled by a grown man, supposedly fairly astute."

He activated the helio-jet and said to his partner, "Okay, there's the list on the screen. Read 'em off."

The patrol car bounded into the air.

They pulled a blank on the first two shops, which were in the near vicinity, somewhat to Tad's surprise. It would seem that even folk who lived in this ritzy neighborhood had the need from time to time to sell, or pawn, their valuables.

They hit it on the third one.

The proprietor, indeed, had a jeweler's magnifying glass screwed into his left eye and was actually examining a ring.

He looked up at their entry and took the glass from his eye and made a wry face. Obviously, he wasn't stupid. They were police.

He said, "What can I do for you, officers?"

Tad gave a quick verbal description of his subject including the clothing he wore. "Did this man come in here and attempt to sell you a ring?"

The other sighed in resignation and handed over the piece of jewelry he had been examining.

"I had a feeling about him," he said defensively.

"I'll bet you did," Jim Kelly said, dripping sarcasm. "What did you give him for it?"

He hesitated but there was no alternative. It would come out. "Three hundred pseudo-dollars."

"Three hundred," Tad said in disgust, examining the diamond. "You drive a hard bargain. It cost two thousand."

"It's a blue diamond, probably from South Africa," the other said in resignation, "but it has a flaw. I might have doubled the price I gave him, if I held it long enough. No more than that."

"What was his name?"

"He said it was Timothy Adams."

"And what was it really?"

"How would I know?"

"And you didn't bother to find out, eh?" Kelly said. "You mean you buy a two thousand buck ring from a stranger without getting identification?"

The shop manager said plaintively, "Look, in this neighborhood, if I pried into the business of my customers they'd go elsewhere. Some of them are supposedly prominent people. They're temporarily short. So they peddle something valuable. But they wouldn't want to have the fact get around." He added, "He was well dressed."

Tad said, "He ought to be. He stole the clothes too. All right. You gave him three hundred pseudo-dollars. To whose account did you transfer the amount?"

"I don't know."

The two policemen eyed him.

He said, still plaintively, "I put my Universal Credit

Card in the credit transfer slot, he put his in. I ordered three hundred pseudo-dollars to be transferred. I didn't see the name on his card.''

Jim said, skepticism there, ''Is that how you usually do it?''

''Yes, confound it. I told you that most of my customers wish to remain incognito. He seemed to be a gentleman.''

Tad said, ''Do you mind if I use your screen? I want to check with the National Data Banks on the credit transfer.''

''Certainly.''

''May I have your Universal Credit Card?''

The man handed it over.

Tad put it in the slot and said, ''Police. Within the past hour, three hundred pseudo-dollars were transferred from this account to another. What was the name and card number of the receiver?''

He got his answer within a minute.

He said into the screen, ''This is Patrolman Tadeusz Boleslaw. If the Universal Credit Card of Rex Moran . . .'' he gave the number ''. . . is utilized, I want an immediate fix on him.''

''Very well, Patrolman Boleslaw,'' the computer voice said.

Tad looked at the ring again and said to Jim, ''Give this gentleman a receipt for it.''

''Hey, wait a minute,'' the shop manager blurted.

Tad looked him over. ''Did you expect to keep it? When we've caught him, we'll transfer the amount back to you.''

''Suppose he's spent some of my three hundred pseudo-dollars?''

''Sue him. You shouldn't be so damned quick to buy

two thousand dollar rings for peanuts. But he won't have the time to spend it.''

Back in the helio-jet again, Jim Kelly said, ''Now what?''

Tad said, ''Now we wait for the stupid funker to try to use that Uni-Credit Card of his. Then we pick him up.''

''Why not call into headquarters and put in a general alarm? They could check out his address and so forth.''

Tad said, ''We can do that later, ourselves, if we want to. This isn't as big as all that. A minor romp. We'll pick him up ourselves and get the credit for it. I suspect that he's still in the neighborhood. And he'll be spending some of that credit shortly. He sounds like a cloddy to me, to be taking chances like this.''

''The old boy said he sounded intelligent.''

''Well, he doesn't act that way.''

VII

Rex Moran now had three hundred pseudo-dollars to his account. That was a damn sight less than he had expected to get. However, he hadn't dared to buy a more expensive piece of jewelry than the two thousand pseudo-dollar piece on Vassilis's credit card. There would have been more of a chance of the shop owner checking on such an item. More chance of it being able to be traced. Besides, if he had drained Vassilis's account too badly, there might have been a computer check at that point.

He walked rapidly for several blocks and found himself in an area with various restaurants. It was just about noon but since he hadn't been able to afford breakfast he was feeling hunger. Well, three hundred pseudo-dollars was three hundred pseudo-dollars and he might as well blow himself to a fairly good repast in an autocafeteria.

He selected one of the better ones and sat himself down at a table and took in the menu listed on the table top. To hell with anything based on Antarctic krill, plankton protein, or soy beans; he was up to some real animal protein and Zoroaster could take the cost.

He put his credit card in the table slot, his thumbprint on the screen and dialed chicken and a mug of sea-booze. He would have liked a shot of pseudo-whiskey to begin, but his funds weren't all that unlimited.

He leaned back and waited for the food and wondered how long it would take for the old mining engineer and his servant to untie themselves. He hoped that it wouldn't take them too long. He didn't have anything against them, now that he had gotten what he wanted.

His pocket transeiver buzzed and he brought it out and scowled at it in surprise. He had it set on Number One priority and only two people in the world were eligible to break in on him on that priority and he certainly wasn't expecting a call from either of them.

He flicked the cover open and looked into the screen.

The face was that of a stranger, squarish and with a very severe expression. The other wore a police cap.

The voice said, "This is Patrolman Boleslaw. Rex Moran, you are under arrest for attempting to violate the regulations pertaining to usage of the Universal Credit Card. Report immediately to the Police Administration Building. Failure to do so will compound the felony."

"Get lost, fuzz-john," Rex Moran snarled. He snapped the instrument off, then stared down at the blank screen in dismay. What had gone wrong? Especially, what had gone wrong so quickly? It had to be something to do with his selling that damned ring. But what? He had expected the ring to stay in that tiny shop, waiting for a customer, for months, perhaps even years. And even then, when it was resold, the transaction should never have appeared on the computer records, except as an exchange of pseudo-dollar credit from the purchaser's account to the shop-keeper's.

What foul luck! Vassilis must have put in an immediate alarm, and the police must have contacted every place in town where Rex Moran could possibly dispose of the purloined ring.

He had to think fast. They'd be after him now. Damn and double damn. He wouldn't even be able to return to his mini-apartment. He was on the run, and for such a meaningless amount as three hundred pseudo-dollars, and even that was now of no use. He wouldn't dare use his credit card; the computers were obviously watching for it to surface.

They could also zero in on his transeiver. He brought it from his pocket and was about to smash it. However, the screen lit up again and a new voice was there.

It rasped, "Now hear this, all citizens. Crimes against the government of the United States of the Americas have been committed by Rex Moran, including assault, robbery, sale of stolen property and attempted misuse of the Universal Credit Card. All citizens are requested to cooperate in his apprehension. The criminal is dangerous and armed with a firearm. Here is his face."

Rex Moran groaned when his face appeared on the tiny screen. Happily, it was a fairly old photo, and taken before some of his present scarred features had become what they were.

He took the transeiver and flung it into a corner. At this early hour there were comparatively few fellow diners in the autocafeteria, thank the living Zoroaster for that. None of them had seemed to spot him, although all, of course, had received the alarm.

He came to his feet and hurried to the door. In the far distance, he could hear a siren. Undoubtedly, it was for him. You didn't hear police sirens that often in the pseudo-cities of the present People's Capitalism state.

He hurried down the street and turned a corner as quickly as possible. He dared not use the vacuum tube metro. The moment he attempted to use his credit card, they'd get a fix on him. He dared not summon an autocab, for that matter.

But that brought something to mind.

He found a fairly isolated spot and waited until a pedestrian came along. He brought his gun from his pocket and said, "Hold it, chum-pal."

The other looked at him, then down to the gun, then into Rex Moran's face again, and blanched. He stuttered, "Why, why you're the criminal just flashed on the transeiver screens."

"That's right, chum-pal, and you look just like the sort of chum-pal who'd cooperate with a man with a shooter trained on his tummy."

The other was wide-eyed and ashen. "Why—why of course. Anything you say."

"Wizard. Quick now, dial an autocab on your transeiver."

"Of course, of course. Don't be nervous." He fumbled his transeiver from a pocket.

"I'm not nervous." Rex Moran grinned at him and jiggled the gun up and down. "Just hurry it up."

The other dialed and within moments an autocab turned the corner and pulled up next to them at the curb. The door opened.

Rex said, "Quick, put your Uni-Credit Card in the slot."

Even as the other was doing so, Moran was climbing into the back seat. He rasped, "Put your thumbprint on the screen." While the other was doing that, Rex Moran was dialing his destination, not letting the other see.

He reached out suddenly and grabbed the other's transeiver and stuck it in his pocket. He pulled the credit card from the autocab's payment slot and handed it back to his victim.

"There," he said, "don't say I didn't do you a favor. Think of all the trouble you'd have if you didn't have your credit card."

He slammed the door shut and the autocab took off.

Rex Moran said into the vehicle's screen, "Maximum speed."

A robot voice said, "Yes, sir."

VIII

Jim Kelly looked over at his sidekick in disgust. "That was a mistake," he said, "trying to arrest him over his transeiver. We should have used the fix we got on his card and come up on him by surprise."

Tad was equally disgusted. He said defensively, "It was standard procedure. He was in a restaurant, and undoubtedly surrounded by other people. Innocent people. The funker's armed. Suppose we'd tried to take him and he'd opened fire and we answered it."

"You'd have a room full of dead people," Jim admitted. "But now he's on the run. He'll try to go to ground."

Tad grunted continued disgust. "Well, he can try till Mercury freezes over, but he'll have his work cut out. You can't live in this society without a Universal Credit Card. You can't buy food, you can't go to a hotel, you can't use public transportation. You can't buy any item or any service. He's sunk."

"Well, I hope the hell he doesn't use that shooter before we pick him up."

Tad sighed and said, "Get on the screen and find out from the data banks where he lives. We'll have the place staked out. Not that it'll do any good. He's not stupid enough to return there."

"He's pretty damn stupid, if you ask me," Jim Kelly muttered, activating the screen.

Tad looked at his wrist chronometer and said, "Our shift's about up, anyway. We'll go in and report to the lieutenant and he can alert all patrol cars. This sort of romp comes under his jurisdiction."

Kelly got the address of Rex Moran's apartment and noted it down with his stylo.

Tad was driving. He headed back for headquarters.

Kelly said, unhappily, "He's on the run. Maybe he'll try to leave Center City. Maybe we better put out a Statewide alert."

"For a romp involving only a few hundred pseudo-dollars, now that we've got the ring back? Besides, he can't leave Center City. He can't use public transportation, and from what Vassilis said about his seedy appearance, it's unlikely he owns a car. Even if he did, he couldn't buy fuel for it. But we'll leave it up to the lieutenant to decide."

Back at the station, the two of them went in to report to Detective Lieutenant Norman Schmidt. He looked up, put down the stylo he'd been using on a report, and rubbed the back of his neck.

The two patrolmen stood there silently for a moment.

Schmidt scowled and said, "You look like you've got something on your minds." He reached for his inevitable beat-up briar and the humidor of tobacco that sat on his desk.

Jim looked at his buddy from the side of his eyes and said, "You tell him."

Tad took a deep breath and went into the report.

When it was through, he stared at them, the stinking pipe going by now.

"Are you two jazzing me?"

They both shook their heads and Tad said, "No, sir."

"You figure this Rex Moran is drivel-happy?"

"Couldn't say."

"It doesn't make any sense at all. I've never even heard of a romp like this since I first made the mistake of becoming a cop." He thought about it. "What kind of a gun did you say he ordered?"

Tad said, "One of those Model C Automatics with that layman's built-in gismo that reports to the data banks and gives a fix on its location every time it's fired."

"I know what a Model C Automatic does," Schmidt growled. "Okay. Go on in to the sergeant and put it all on the air. His name, his Uni-Credit Card number, Vassilis's card number. Alert every patrol car in the city. He won't last for more than a few hours, no matter how smart he thinks he is."

Tad and Jim left to obey orders. The lieutenant sighed and picked up his stylo again.

After their report, which left the sergeant as unbelieving as it had the lieutenant, Tad and Jim went into the dressing rooms and to their lockers and got out of their uniforms and into civilian clothes.

"See you in the morning, Jim," Tad said, taking off.

He went down to the corner metro station and took the vacuum tube to the building in which he resided and then the elevator up to his mini-apartment.

Once there, he slumped into his comfort chair.

The fact was, he couldn't forget Charles Brothers, in spite of the excitement of the chase of the offbeat Rex Moran. Buddy Brothers kept nagging at him. The whole thing didn't ring true. Okay, what Norm Schmidt had said was believable. The guy was a war hero who had won medals and wasn't about to truckle to a bunch of cheap hoods. He went armed and provided with a police emergency wrist alarm and he was ready and able to take on anybody who gave him trouble. But something still didn't quite ring true. In all, Brothers had killed four of these young funkers. Four! He hadn't simply wounded a single one. All were dead by the time the police got to the scene. Of course, using a gyro-jet rocket pistol would account for that. But still. Four. In all of his police years, Tad Boleslaw had killed exactly one man. And he was sorry about that. He should have been able to bring the other down without killing him. A prowler had run up an alley with Tad in full pursuit. It proved to be a dead end. The man turned and pulled a gun. Tad tried to wing him but he shot too hurriedly, under the pressure, the possibility that the other would shoot first, and got him in the belly. The ambulance, for once, took hell's own time to get to the scene. Everything went wrong. The poor bastard was DOA at the hospital.

Of course, Tad had nicked several others in his time, some of them pretty badly, but he had only killed the one. But four, in the holy name of Zoroaster, and the man wasn't even a real cop.

Since he was a bachelor and impatient of larger quarters, Tad lived in a mini-apartment in a moderately sized high-rise apartment house. There were some five hundred apartments in the building and he doubted if he knew half a dozen of the people who were supposedly his neighbors. It suited him and his way of life, but he knew that this existence was rapidly becoming unpopular with most. Too ant-like.

The big cities were breaking up and the inhabitants, like

lemmings, were streaking out into the boondocks, some to small communities, some to an even more isolated existence, or mobile towns. People's Capitalism, as some called it, allowed for not only Inalienable Basic dividends but also provided each family in the land one free residence, or mobile home. In actuality, you could apply for yours, get it—there was a certain maximum amount of pseudo-dollars you were allowed to expend, according to the size of the family—and then sell it the very next day, if you wished. But from then on you either had to buy another place on your own, or rent. There was a certain method in the seeming madness. It was a way of counterbalancing the fall-off economically when so much of the military spending had been discontinued. The billions formerly expended on so-called defense were put into construction and into other fields such as ecology and the rebuilding of the environment.

All for the best, he assumed, although Tad Boleslaw was precious little interested in such subjects as socioeconomics. He was a dedicated cop and a good one. He found it a satisfactory manner of making a living, though unromantic, usually drab and laborious. He had a moderately good education and had also had two tours at the Intercontinental Bureau of Investigation school. He studied every issue of such technical publications as *Criminology*, *Police Science*, and the *Journal of Criminal Law*. He had a distinguished marksman rating, and two citations on his record. After training, he had moved up from probation through the two patrolman grades and had his fingers crossed about getting detective status in the reasonably near future.

It was getting along in the day. He got up and went over

to his autobar and began to dial. But then he thought the hell with the ersatz guzzle that was the ordinary fare. Instead, he turned to the little buffet next to the bar and selected one of the precious bottles there. Polish vodka, real vodka. He poured a generous portion into one of his liquor glasses, and carried it into his so-called kitchenette, sat down at the small table and dialed dinner from the automated kitchens in the basement of the building. And thank the holy Zoroaster for them, too. He was the type that couldn't even brew a decent cup of coffee.

He was so preoccupied with his thinking about Charles Brothers that he didn't taste his food and his vodka, and was mildly surprised to find the meal was over. He threw the dishes and utensils into the disposal and turned back into the livingroom-cum-bedroom.

He got a refill on the vodka, went over to his desk and dialed the National Data Banks on his screen.

He said verbally, rather than dialing for his information, "I want the Dossier Complete of Charles Brothers." He opened his police notebook and flicked to the page he had used the night before and read off the identification code of his subject.

The screen said, "What is your classification, please? Are you eligible to request a citizen's Dossier Complete?"

"Police officer," he said, and put his identification card on the appropriate square of the screen.

And there was the life of Charles Brothers.

Very cold was a citizen's dossier, very sterile. But all the information was there. Had Tad been interested, he could have found out about grandparents, parents, date of birth, doctor presiding at birth, health from his earliest years, every time he had medical attention, every childhood disease from the first months, every other visit to a doctor, up to and through any venereal disease he might have picked up in Asia during the war, etc.

Brothers had a high school education as they had called it in those days. Evidently, an average student. As a matter of fact, he seemed average all ways from Tuesday. Tad got to the war years. His subject had been drafted and had seemingly been a good soldier, rising to the rank of sergeant. He had spent four years in the infantry, which would seem to be plenty.

And then Tad Boleslaw came to his first discrepancy. Charles Brothers' military discharge status was blank.

That seemed strange. He flicked a switch and said, "What type of discharge was Charles Brothers given?" He repeated the other's identification code.

The screen said, "That information is restricted."

Tad blinked. He said, "Why?"

"That information is also restricted."

He'd be damned. He went on with the dossier. Following the war, Brothers had taken training in the category tabulating, specializing on IBM machines. He had seemingly been good at it and got promotions. He was currently being paid three hundred pseudo-dollars a week as a shift supervisor in an installation in an ultra-market.

Three hundred pseudo-dollars a week! And living in a dump like that? Well, not really a dump. The apartment was pleasant enough, once you got inside it. But in that cheap ghetto? That slum?

He went on. Married. Divorced a couple of years ago. One child. Tilly.

Yes, Tilly. The scared girl. Scared of what?

He ran into his second surprise. Organizations to which

the other belonged. Brothers had applied to join the National Guard. Application refused. Reason restricted.

Application refused! To a war hero?

He sunk back into his chair for a moment, then flicked his switch again and said, ''What classification is needed to receive the information about Charles Brothers' military discharge and his application refusal to join the National Guard?''

''A Military Classification One.''

One! Holy Jumping Zoroaster, you practically had to be a member of the Chiefs of Staff, or the President himself. One! Who in the hell was this Brothers?

He had largely skim-read but now he had come to the end of the dossier. He leaned back in his chair, finished his vodka and stared at the screen for a time.

Then he said into it, ''I want the crime dossier of Charles Brothers.''

''What is your classification, please? Are you eligible to read a citizen's crime dossier?''

He went through that routine again.

And there was the crime dossier.

There was precious little that Tad Boleslaw didn't already know, aside from a couple of traffic violations before the war and one drunk and disorderly charge back when Brothers had been eighteen. He came to the subject's military years. A.W.O.L. once for two days. Another minor offense whilst going through training; he had refused to obey an order by one of his non-coms. Tad didn't bother to read the details.

He then came to another surprise. There were a lot of militarized numbers and references and general gobbledygook and then a stamp, *Information Restricted*.

That stopped him momentarily but then he went back to the crime dossier of Charles Brothers following the Asian War.

It was nil except for the four shootings. The first two had been Blacks, as Tad had already known. They were brothers, Wilbur and Washington Scott, eighteen and twenty years old, respectively, both with lengthy crime records. The third, Jesus Martinez, a Cuban of 18 years, had no particular record. Schmidt had already told him that. The third shooting, that of the other night, was Jose Gonzales, a Mexican.

And that was the crime career, such as it was, of Charles Brothers.

Tad thought about it awhile and then requested the crime dossier of Jose Gonzales. Though of Mexican background, he had been born in Arizona. His record was sparse. As a twelve-year-old he had been picked up by the juvenile authorities for pilfering candy in an ultra-market. He had been properly scolded and released. He had been picked up again at fifteen for loitering, evidently in the companionship of less savory young friends. About a year ago he had been arrested while riding in a stolen car. It turned out that he hadn't known it was stolen. The driver, who had given him a ride, had ripped off the vehicle. Jose was turned loose. And that was all, no more crime record.

Tad slumped back again.

The boy that Brothers had shot the other night had, for all practical purposes, no criminal record at all. Tad probably had one that was worse. Although now that he thought about it, he had never looked up his own dossier. He probably had a few traffic violations, or somesuch, to his credit. Oh, yes, and that time he was in the peace demonstration while in college. He had been arrested along with a score of other students and released when the Civil Liberties Union hit the ceiling.

He turned off his screen awhile and thought about it, then turned it back on and asked for the military dossier on Charles Brothers.

It would seem that he *had* been a war hero. Besides his Bronze Star, which wasn't easily acquired and was taken in combat, he had several battle stars, a few campaign ribbons—but anybody could get those—and three Purple Hearts. In other words, the innocuous-appearing Buddy Brothers, as Jim Kelly had called him, had been hit by enemy fire three times.

The last item was what stopped him. It was practically a duplication of the restricted information in the Dossier Complete he had first read. Something had happened. Tad hadn't the slightest clue as to what. A court martial, or something? The report didn't even give that.

Charles Brothers was discharged. Period. Honorably? Dishonorably? Medical? For being a homosexual? Or what? The information simply wasn't there.

Suddenly, he became irritated with himself. This was a hell of a way to spend his time. He and Jim Kelly worked a full four-day week. Why should he devote his free time to worrying about something that wasn't really his concern? Charles Brothers had been exonerated. To hear Norm Schmidt talk, the bemedaled veteran should get another medal for knocking off undesirable juvenile delinquents. Maybe he was right. Zoroaster knew, there were enough of them these days. What with automation and computerization of industry and distribution, it was practically impossible to get a job any more and the streets were overflowing with delinquent kids. But that didn't give them a mandate to prey on their elders.

He flicked off his screen and came to his feet, yawning. He went over to his small bar and dialed an ersatz Scotch and soda and when it was delivered went over with it to his comfort chair and took a sip. He'd finish this and then go to bed.

He scowled down into his glass, wondering if real whiskey would ever come back. Probably not, so long as Production Planning refused to allow barley or other cereals to be used in its making. They made this stuff from seaweed or something, didn't they? He wished the hell he had treated himself to some of his private bottled stuff rather than utilizing the autobar. Decent guzzle was really prohibitively expensive, but it was practically his only luxury.

IX

Rex Moran realized that he could not stay in the autocab for very long. Just enough time to get out of this neighborhood. As soon as that cloddy he had just stuck up back there reported to the police, they'd check through the computers for the vehicle's destination. There'd be a record based on the number of the victim's Uni-Credit Card. A record of seemingly everything went into the computer banks. "Why not?" he growled; their capacity was infinite.

Yes, they'd check the destination of his trip. However, he was not quite so silly as to go all the way to the destination he had dialed. About halfway there, at a traffic control stop, he opened the door and left the autocab to go on on its own.

He ducked through a side street and took off at right angles to the avenue along which the cab was progressing.

Rex Moran now had a double problem. He grimaced wryly. An immediate double problem, that was. For one thing, he was still hungry. For another, he had to get off the streets. Citizens weren't apt to pay much attention to the police calls over the transeiver hookup but there was always the exception. Given time, someone would spot him and report him, in spite of the poor photograph which had just been broadcast.

He could hear the stolen transeiver buzz in his pocket and brought it forth, flicking the tiny stud which prevented it from transmitting his face.

It was the same official as before and he was making the same broadcast, but now reporting Rex Moran as last being seen in that part of town where he had dialed the autocab. Evidently, his victim had reported.

That meant also that they would know that Moran had the stolen transeiver and would shortly be zeroing in on it. The computers could get a fix on any citizen's transeiver. He threw the gadget into the gutter and ground a heel down on it.

He simply had to get off the streets.

And suddenly he knew where to go.

In this vicinity there was a posh restaurant of which he had heard but had never been able to afford, nor had he really ever expected to be able to afford. Well, things were different now.

He entered the building and took the elevator to the penthouse restaurant known as the Gourmet Room. The day was more advanced now, and upper-class office workers were beginning to stream in for the mid-day meal.

He avoided looking impressed at the ostentatious swank of this rendezvous of the ultra-wealthy and thanked his stars that he had thought of acquiring his present expensive clothing. A headwaiter approached diffidently. In all his life, Rex Moran had never eaten in a restaurant which boasted live waiters. Now he continued to try to look unimpressed.

"A single, sir?" the maître d' said.

"Please," Rex Moran told him, keeping his voice softly modulated and as though such surroundings were an everyday affair for him. "If possible, a table set back somewhere. I have a bit of figuring to do."

"Certainly, sir. This way."

He was seated in an out-of-the-way alcove which suited his needs perfectly.

The maître d' snapped his fingers and a waiter scurried up.

There was no menu. It was that kind of a restaurant.

The maître d' said unctuously, "Sir, today the *gratin de langoustines Georgette* is superb."

Rex Moran hadn't the vaguest idea what *langoustines Georgette* might be, but he made a face as though considering.

"What else might you recommend?" he said.

"The chef has surpassed himself with the *poulet Docteur*."

"That sounds good."

The waiter made a note.

"And a half bottle of sylvaner of the Haut-Rhine, perhaps? The manager was able to lay down a sizable cellar before Central Production disallowed the production of grapes for beverages."

"Fine."

Salad and dessert were settled upon and then the maître d' hotel and the waiter were gone.

Rex Moran sighed inwardly and looked around. The only other diner within his immediate vicinity had his back to him.

He unslung the Poloroid-Pentax camera from his shoulder and brought from his pocket the cassette of film. He inserted it in the camera. Then he took from his inner pocket the Universal Credit Card he had appropriated from Frank Vassilis and examined it with care, spending particular time on the thumbprint.

Finally, he propped the card against the small vase in the table center, which held a single black rose, and focused the camera on it. He clicked the shutter, then drew the photo from the camera back and stared at it. It didn't quite do. He tried again, getting the camera closer to the subject. He took half a dozen shots before he came up with as near a duplication of the Universal Credit Card's thumbprint as he could hope for.

He put the credit card away, the camera back in its case, and brought forth his pocketknife. He was busily trimming the photo to be the exact size of a thumbprint when the waiter turned up with his first course.

Poulet Docteur turned out to be the best chicken dish he had ever tasted. And the wine was excellent.

In the middle of his salad course, and before dessert, he came suddenly to his feet and hurried toward the reception desk-cum-cashier's booth. It was there that the payment screen for the ultra-swank restaurant was to be found.

And it was there that the maître d' stood, his eyebrows politely raised now.

Rex Moran said to him hurriedly, "I have just thought of something I must attend to. Please hold my dessert for me. And, please, keep an eye on my camera, over there, will you?"

The maître d' looked over at Moran's table. The expensive camera sat upon it. He said, "Why, of course, sir."

Rex Moran left, still projecting an air of suddenly remembering a matter urgent that must be taken care of.

Down on the street he grimaced. One camera sacrificed to the game. However, he had no need of it now.

He was still in one of the best sections of town. He made his way toward a nearby hotel, the New Carlton, holding his handkerchief over his face, as though trying to extract something from his left eye. There were quite a few pedestrians at this time of the day.

In the hotel, he approached the lone clerk at the reception desk. Now he had to take his chances. If the man recognized him from the police broadcast, Rex Moran was on the spot.

He said, "I would like a small suite. Nothing ambitious. Living room, bedroom, bath. I doubt if I shall be entertaining."

"Why, yes sir, of course." The other looked beyond Moran. "Ah, your luggage, sir?"

"I have no luggage," Rex Moran said, off-handedly. "I just came in from the Coast. Plan to do some shopping here for my wardrobe. Always buy my things here in the East. California styles are ludicrous."

"Yes, sir, of course." The clerk motioned in the direction of the slot on the desk. "Would you wish to register?"

"I'd rather see the suite before deciding," Rex Moran said. "I'll register up there, if it's satisfactory."

"Oh, I'm sure it will be, sir. Let me suggest Suite Double A."

"Double A," Rex Moran said and made his way to the bank of elevators. The New Carlton was swank enough to have a live receptionist clerk, but evidently not so un-automated as to boast bellhops.

Inside the first elevator, he said, "Suite Double A."

"Yes, sir," a robot voice said.

Suite Double A was several stories up. Rex Moran emerged from the elevator, looked up at the direction signs on the wall and made his way to the suite in question. The identity screen on the door picked him up and the door opened. Evidently, the clerk below was on his toes.

It was quite the most elaborate quarters in which Rex Moran had ever been. Not that that was the issue. He would have taken the accommodations whatever they had resembled.

He approached the room's phone screen, flicked it on, and, yawning, said, "I'll take it. The suite seems adequate."

"Very good, sir," the clerk in the screen said, beaming. "Would you like to register now."

Rex Moran yawned again and said, "I'll take care of it in the morning. I'm tired. I'll be here at least a week."

The clerk looked hesitant momentarily, but then said, "Very good, sir." His face faded.

Rex Moran let out a breath in relief. That had been the crucial point. If the clerk had insisted on immediate registration, then Moran would have had to have gotten huffy and left, to try the same thing elsewhere. On the face of it, he had no luggage, and hence should be suspect. However, the New Carlton was no cheap pad. Rex Moran was most expensively attired. The clerk was in no position to antagonize wealthy customers.

He dialed the time. It was mid-afternoon.

He grinned exuberantly. He had it licked. Unless there was something he didn't know about, he absolutely had it licked.

He dialed service and said into the screen, "I'd like to lay in a stock of potables. Let me see. Let's say a bottle of Scotch, one of Cognac, one of Metaxa, one of Benedictine, one of Cherry Herring, one of Chartreuse—yellow, of course, not the green—one of Pernod, absinthe if available, but otherwise the ordinary will do.''

"Sir," a robot voice said, "in the New Carlton all these can be dialed on the autobar."

"I know, I know," Rex Moran said impatiently. "But I like to mix my own."

"Very good, sir. They will be delivered through the autobar, sir."

"Mind," Rex Moran said, "the very best quality. I don't wish any of this modern stuff."

"Always, sir."

Still grinning widely, he went over to the suite's autobar and waited for the guzzle to be delivered. He took up the bottle of Glengrant Scotch and held it up to the light approvingly. In his whole life he had been drenched exactly twice on real Scotch, left over from the old days. The stuff was worth its weight in rubies since Central Production had discontinued the use of cereals for distillations.

He dialed for soda and ice and sipped away at the Scotch approvingly, even as he strode up and down the room, considering his immediate future.

He wondered briefly how you went about getting a mopsy up to your quarters in a hostelry as posh as the New Carlton. But he had better draw the line there, anyway. It was no use pushing your luck. Some wheel might come off. She might have seen the police alarm on him.

Prostitution hadn't been completely abolished under People's Capitalism, but it had certainly altered since the world's first profession had been instituted. There was no manner in which the john could pay off in pseudo-dollars, so the girls were in the way of being semi-amateurs. They peddled their artificial love for *things*, rather than money. A girl who had to live on her Inalienable Basic dividends, and who dreamed of the nicer things of life, could peddle her alleged virtue in return for gifts: jewelry, clothes she couldn't ordinarily afford, meals and entertainment in restaurants and nightclubs she couldn't begin to afford.

But no. No matter how amusing it might have been to have an alleged fallen woman or two up to his suite, he had to be *somewhat* careful.

What the hell else was there in the way of unrealized lifelong ambitions?

Caviar. He had never had his fill of caviar. In fact, the amount of caviar he had eaten in his whole life could have come out of a two ounce jar of the precious stuff. The Soviet Complex and Iran, these days, doled it out as though it were diamonds, rather than fish eggs. At a cocktail party, you'd find three or four eggs on a canape.

Wizard. He dialed service again and had a pound jar of caviar sent up, along with sweet butter, toast, chopped eggs and chopped onion. While he was at it, he ordered a sizable amount of smoked sturgeon and smoked salmon.

While he was awaiting this order, he built himself another Scotch and soda. Glengrant. He'd have to remember that name, on the off chance, which was pretty off, that he'd ever have another opportunity such as this.

He spent the rest of the day indulging himself in every food and drink ambition he could ever remember having had—and in getting well-drenched and surfeited with rich edibles to the point that when dinner time arrived, he had no appetite, to his disgust. He had wanted to order a real gargantuan meal.

His last memory was of staggering into the bedroom and dialing the bed to ultimate softness before throwing himself into it. Now he had second thoughts about locating a mopsy.

X

In the morning Rex Moran should have awakened with some sort of hangover, but the holy Zoroaster was still with him; either that, or there was another good mark to chalk up for Glengrant Scotch. He awoke grinning at the ceiling. He had slept like a log.

He dialed the time at the bedside phone screen and didn't bother to look into it. A robot voice said, "When the bell rings it will be exactly nine minutes to eight hours."

Ha! Nine minutes to go.

He dialed breakfast, a monstrous breakfast, and had it delivered to the auto-table next to the bed. Fresh mango juice, papaya, eggs in black butter, caviar again, toast, fried tomatoes, coffee; double orders of all.

Groaning satisfaction, he ate.

By the time breakfast was over it was well past eight o'clock.

Wizard, he grinned jubilantly. It was time to get busy.

He went to the phone screen after toilet and dialed the local branch of the ultra-market and men's furnishings. He took his time selecting a new change of clothing. That accomplished, he dialed the order, put Vassilis's Universal Credit Card in the slot and laid the photo of the thumbprint on the screen and took it off immediately.

The clothing arrived in minutes, and he dressed with great care. He had already showered and shaved in the well-equipped bathroom.

He returned to the phone screen and dialed the ultra-market once again. He began ordering items in fine discrimination and had the time of his life unwrapping and examining them as they arrived. He ordered wrist chronometers, sports equipment, clothes, paintings, other art, everything he could think of. His loot piled up.

At about nine o'clock he decided to do it up brown and dialed a floater sales outlet. He ordered a sports model private floater and instructed them to send it over to the hotel's parking lot on automatic.

XI

At ten minutes after nine, the identity screen on the door lit up. There were two men there, both in uniform, police uniform. Rex Moran pressed the button which activated the door and they entered, watching him warily.

Moran grinned at them and said, ''Where've you been?''

The younger one said, ''Rex Moran?''

Moran was grinning still. He said, ''That's one of the pseudonyms I go by.''

The policeman said, ''Don't be a cloddy. There is no such thing as a pseudonym any more, the data banks are too accurate. You can't start up a false identity.''

''You'd be surprised.''

''I'm Patrolman Boleslaw, and this is Patrolman Kelly. You're under arrest. Where's the gun?''

Even as Tad spoke, his hand, as it had ever since he had entered the room, was near his quick-drawn holster with its .38 Recoilless. With someone as drivel-happy as this, you couldn't afford to take chances.

''Over there on the table,'' Rex Moran said, he gestured with a cock of his head.

Jim Kelly went over and picked the weapon up. He expertly flicked the stud that released the magazine from the butt.

In surprise, he said to Tad, "It's not loaded." He stuck it in a side pocket, after returning the clip to its place.

Moran said, "I wasn't expecting to shoot it."

Tad eyed him, and said, "What were you expecting to do with it?"

"I'll never tell," Moran said mockingly.

Jim Kelly looked about the room, at all the purchases, the wrapping paper and string strewn everywhere. There were fishing rods and shotguns, men's jewelry and books, bottles of guzzle and even a couple of paintings. It was a meaningless hodgepodge.

"Zoroaster," Kelly snorted. "He's as far around the bend as you can get."

They took him down the elevator, through the lobby and out to the street where their patrol car was parked. Jim Kelly got behind the controls and Tad climbed into the back with Moran.

Before taking off, Jim flicked on the screen and said, "Kelly and Boleslaw. We picked up Rex Moran and are bringing him in. You can call the rest of the boys off."

"Will do," the corporal on the screen said.

They zoomed up, heading for headquarters.

Tad Boleslaw looked at their prisoner in disgust and said, "You must have had the time of your life. What are you bucking for, a stay at the Psychotherapy Institute?"

Rex Moran laughed.

"Big joke," Tad growled. "We could have nabbed you there in the autocafeteria. We could have zeroed in on you instead of trying to arrest you by transeiver."

"I wondered why you didn't," Rex Moran said. "Police inefficiency?"

"We didn't know how trigger-happy you might be," Tad told him.

At headquarters they took him directly to Lieutenant Schmidt's office.

Schmidt looked up and took the prisoner in interestedly. "Got him, eh? How'd it work out?"

"He'd holed up in the New Carlton Hotel last night, not immediately registering. By the way, a report ought to be made to the management about the clerk who allowed him to do it. If he'd used either of the two Uni-Credit Cards he was carrying to register we would have gotten an immediate fix on him and could have rounded him up at that time. The law is that a guest has to register, using his card, for identification, upon admission to a hotel."

"I know what the law is," Schmidt told him. "Sometimes they wink at it, especially in the swankier hotels. Suppose you were married and had a different mopsy with you. At any rate, take him up to the commissioner's office, right away."

Tad looked at him, his face blank. "The Commissioner's office? Don't you want us to book him first? And what would the commissioner care about . . ."

Schmidt went back to his papers, saying wearily, "Maybe he'll tell you. I didn't hear the full story until an hour ago."

Shrugging his lack of understanding, Tad led the way, followed by the grinning Rex Moran, with Jim Kelly bringing up the rear.

They took the elevator up to the third floor and proceeded, still in file, to the reception room of Commissioner Marvin Ruhling. The sergeant receptionist at the desk there motioned them in with a jerk of his thumb and without speaking.

Tad Boleslaw had been in this rarefied atmosphere but

once before, when he had received his badge upon graduation from police school. Marvin Ruhling made a point of personally interviewing each new patrolman and giving him a stereotype pep talk. In Tad's opinion the place looked more like the office of an international tycoon, rather than what you would expect of Center City's top cop.

There was one other person there, not recognized by either of the two patrolmen. He was a starched type, somewhere in his mid-forties, was conservatively though expensively dressed, radiated authority and right now wore an air of irritation.

He looked at Rex Moran and said, "Very funny, ordering even a sports floater."

Rex Moran laughed and took a comfortable chair. Tad and Jim ogled him. And then Jim stepped forward as though to jerk Moran back to his feet.

Commissioner Ruhling said, "That'll be all, ah, Kelly, isn't it?"

Kelly came to a halt and blinked further surprise.

The commissioner said, "This is Mr. Warren Hammond, of the banking section of the National Data Banks Uh, let me see, Patrolmen Boleslaw and Kelly, isn't it?"

Hammond nodded distantly at the introduction but his disgusted eyes were still on Moran.

Hammond said, "What kind of a mess do you think Frank Vassilis is going to stir up?"

Rex Moran said reasonably, "I suggest that nobody ever let him know what happened. Return his Universal Credit Card and restore his credit in the data banks. He wasn't done any harm. He had a little excitement, and from what I saw of the old boy, probably enjoyed it."

Tad and Jim were bug-eyeing back and forth between the two speakers.

"A little excitement, you cloddy. Suppose he had dropped dead from a heart attack or something," Hammond rapped in irritation. "Not to mention that pedestrian you forced at gun point to get an auto-cab for you."

Moran said easily, crossing his legs, "Well, you asked for it. You wanted authenticity. You got it."

"Authenticity!" Commissioner Ruhling muttered. Then, "Which reminds me. We better have that broadcast killed, or the next time Rex goes out on the street, somebody'll shoot him."

Tad blurted, "You mean that this is all a fake, a put-up job?"

They ignored him.

Warren Hammond said, in resignation, "Well, what are your conclusions, Rex? Center City is supposed to be the average city of the nation. Anything that could happen here could happen anywhere."

Rex Moran turned off the humor he had been expressing ever since the two patrolmen had picked him up and said seriously, "We've got to do something to the cards. Something to guarantee that the thumbprint is legitimate. Otherwise, a real bad-o could locate some upperclass cloddy without any immediate friends or relatives, take him out somewhere in the boondocks and finish him off and hide the body. Then he'd take the Uni-Credit Card and head into some other part of the country and, using the same system I did, duplicate photographically the thumbprint. And for the rest of his life he could milk the dividends that would accrue on his victim's credit account from his shares of Variable Basic."

Hammond said, looking at him sharply, "What could we do to the credit cards?"

"Search me," Moran said. "That's up to the engineers. Maybe something in the cards, or on the screens, to detect body heat. I don't know. But I proved that the Universal Credit Card is vulnerable the way it is."

"What else?" Hammond demanded of someone who was obviously one of his troubleshooters.

Rex Moran thought about it and looked at the police commissioner. He said, "Sir, that system of making a citizen arrest himself and turning himself over to the nearest police station doesn't wash. I know that it's just an experiment being tried out here in the most average city in the country. But it doesn't wash. Oh, I'll admit it saves manpower, ordinarily, and would work with the average honest citizen. But when you get some funker vicious enough to be carrying a shooter, then you should zero in on his transeiver, assuming he's stupid enough to be carrying one, or his credit card, without warning."

Hammond looked over at the commissioner. "This is out of my field, and no concern to me, but Rex is obviously right on that."

"Ummm," the commissioner said thoughtfully. "It's only an experiment, as he said, of course. This poor town is used to test out every experiment that the double domes dream up."

Hammond sighed deeply and came back to Rex Moran. "All right," he said. "You won your bet. You were able to beat the rap, exist in comfort for a full twenty-four hours, without any pseudo-dollar credits."

He glared at his trouble-shooter. "But I'd sure as the holy living Zoroaster like to see you do it six months from now, when I've cleared up some of those loopholes you used.''

Rex Moran grinned at him. "It's a bet," he said. He came to his feet and with a *friendly* grin this time came over to Tad and Jim with an extended hand. "It was a pleasure to work with you fellows," he said.

"Thanks," Tad said bitterly.

XII

Heading down for the dressing room and lockers on the ground floor, Jim said, "I still don't know what in the hell that was all about."

Tad said, "It's simple enough. Haven't you ever heard of Warren Hammond?"

"I don't think so."

"He's top man in the banking section of the Universal Credit Cards. They keep the books. They're also in charge of issuing every citizen his ten shares of Inalienable Basic Common Stock, of these our United States of the Americas, upon birth, and also in charge of selling to any citizen who can afford them, shares of Variable Basic. And they're in charge of deciding how much the dividends will be and crediting each citizen his amount based on how many shares he holds in all."

"I know all that," Jim said, as they entered the elevator, "but what in the hell was that with Rex Moran?"

"Every would-be sharpy in the country is continually trying to figure out some way of beating the rap. Some way of getting more out of his credit account than there is in it. Some way of jimmying his Universal Credit Card. And some of them evidently come up with real wizards. So Hammond's department is continually faced with new brainstorms. In this case it would seem that Rex Moran bet his boss that he could figure out some way of living in luxury without anything at all in his credit account.

"They outfitted him with a phony name—remember he told us that Rex Moran was a pseudonym—and a phony set of identification papers, transeiver, and probably even a phony dossier and put him down here in Center City without any pseudo-dollars. To make it authentic, they even fixed him up with an apartment. And then he started out to make Center City's police look like fools. And he did. No wonder he was laughing when we picked him up."

They had arrived at their lockers.

Jim was shaking his head. "What a way to make a living," he said. Tad didn't bother to ask him if he was referring to being a cop, or speaking of Rex Moran.

Jim said, "Tomorrow we got off. What're you going to do, Tad?" Jim Kelly was skinning out of his tunic.

"Get drunk."

"Why don't you come over to the house and have dinner with me and Molly and the kids?"

"Thanks, Jim, but no thanks. I'm feeling frustrated. First that Buddy Brothers thing, now this."

"What about Brothers?" Jim said, pulling his civilian suit from the locker.

"I don't know. That's what's frustrating," Tad grumbled. "See you the day after tomorrow, Jim. I'm really going to hang one on."

Jim looked at him, his face worried. He said, "Tad, why in the hell don't you find some nice girl and settle down?"

Tad grunted and said, "I don't like nice girls. I like bad girls better. They put out easier. So long, Jim."

Tad slept as late into the morning as he usually did when he was on the night shift. It was a habit he couldn't shake. When, as he had been for the past few days, they put him on a temporary day shift, he couldn't recondition himself to different sleeping hours. He went to bed late, got up late.

He had breakfast, tried to read one of his police manuals for awhile, gave up. He was at loose ends and rather wished that he had taken Jim up on his dinner invitation. Tad liked Molly Kelly and could even tolerate the two children. On top of that, Molly was an anachronism; she cooked her own meals. It was a definite change from the food from the automated kitchens that Tad was used to. She occasionally burned something, or got it too salty, or whatever. So far as he was concerned, great. He'd always been of the opinion that cooking was a field that should never have been automated. He felt the same way about his guzzle. When he drank martinis, for instance, sometimes he felt like having them drier, sometimes stronger in vermouth. Sometimes he wanted two or three olives, rather than one. On top of everything else, he loathed ersatz vermouth, which was invariably utilized in auto-bar drinks.

He thought about Jim's suggestion that he get married. He was getting to an age where you were usually more settled down than he was. He wondered if his being single kept him from promotion, if the powers that be wanted more settled types. He was uncomfortable with the idea, but doubted it. He simply didn't have the seniority to make detective sergeant.

Being married would have its advantages. For instance, even if his wife didn't work she would have her Inalienable Basic dividends from the government and they'd be able to pool their incomes and, among other things, afford a larger apartment than this mini he now occupied. However, that was a helluva reason to get married—for the sake of a larger apartment.

He decided to go on down town to The Mall and see if anything was stirring. He could have called one of his feminine friends but simply didn't feel like it. He was in an unhappy frame of mind.

Instead of summoning an autocab from the car pool on the third basement floor, he went on down to the metro and took the vacuum tube into Center City. There were too many vehicles around as it was.

In The Mall he sauntered about. When he had been a youngster, there had been a good many small shops here. But that was yesteryear. With the coming of the ultra-market, the small shop had begun to wither away. You could order anything, but anything, in your own home and have it delivered there into your delivery box by vacuum chute almost instantly. Why spend time shopping? The ultra-market was a combination of the large mail order houses, such as Sears and Roebuck, of the past, and the most super of supermarkets and the vacuum-chute delivery combined with the Universal Credit Card seemingly solved all buying problems.

The Mall, these days, aside from being a charming, traffic-free area for loafing away on a bench, or strolling about amongst begging pigeons, watching the girls go by, and such, boasted various bars and restaurants, usually highly specialized; Chinese, Italian, French, Mexican. You could, of course, have ordered any of the dishes in the privacy of your own home, from the building's automated kitchens, but some citizens liked the congenial atmosphere of a well-done restaurant. There were also art galleries, theatres for live shows, nightclubs and various other public establishments purveying items or entertainment not very practical to purchase in the privacy of the home.

He stopped for a few minutes and stared into the window of an art gallery. He peered down at the name of the artist, Josh Rhinedorf. Tad had never heard of him. His style seemed to be a return to the Impressionists.

There was someone standing next to him.

He looked up and said, "Why, it's Ms. Brothers. Good afternoon."

She blinked her blue eyes through the slightly pink tinted lenses of her glasses. She was small in stature, he realized now, as he hadn't particularly in her home—size six, at a guess. And she looked even nicer than she had before, though she wore no cosmetics whatsoever and her clothes were, once again, long years out of date. Not that Tad Boleslaw was any fanatic about women's styles.

She said, in her small voice, "Oh yes, Mr . . . "

"Boleslaw," he reminded her, smiling. "My partner and I returned your father's gun the other night. Tad Boleslaw."

"Yes, of course," she said, and then looked up and down the street as though seeking some reason for departure.

But Tad wasn't having any. There was an elfin something about this girl that attracted him. And there was also a—well, he couldn't exactly quite put his finger on it. A mystery of some sort or other. There was something about her. . . .

He said, "It's one of my days off. I'm just killing time. The Hole is just up the street. Would you join me?"

"The Hole?"

He laughed. "Sam's Bar. Really, a very nice place. Sam owns one of the few unautomated bars in town and serves the best dark beer I've ever tasted. He has everything else, too, of course, if you don't like beer."

"Oh, Father doesn't permit me to drink intoxicants," she told him.

He took her in, his head tilted to one side a little. The girl was twenty-five or so, he would say.

He said, "For that matter, Sam carries soft drinks. You could have a Del Valle, or something, while I had my beer and we could find out a little about each other."

She said, her voice wavering just a bit, "What did you want to find out about me, Mr. Boleslaw?"

He stared at her, set back, and said, "Why, nothing. I meant that . . . well, I just thought that we could chat a little."

"I'm afraid that my father wouldn't approve of my entering an establishment where they served hard drink."

He was exasperated but hid it and said, "Well, then, we'll go somewhere where they serve only soft drinks and we'll both have a Del Valle."

She said—and was there a distant regret there?—"I don't think my father would approve of me associating with a man to whom I haven't been properly introduced. Forgive me, and thank you. Good afternoon, Mr. Boleslaw." She turned and made off.

He gazed after her. Her long brown hair bounced charmingly on her shoulders and the very faint sway of her buttocks gave promise of a fascinating figure under those antiquated clothes.

"Properly introduced, for Zoroaster's sake?" he muttered under his breath. "I was introduced to you in your own home by your own father. How proper can an introduction get?"

In disgust, though why he should be bothered he couldn't say, he went on up the way to The Hole and took a stool at the bar. He liked the place. It was his favorite bar. Sam had made every effort to create an atmosphere of the type that had prevailed before World War I, a century ago. It was pleasantly dim, pleasantly cool, though without air conditioning which was all right with Tad who disliked the artificial cold of air conditioning.

Sam came down and, without orders, began to draw a dark beer.

Tad said, "Sam, how old do you figure a girl should be before she's allowed to drink, enter bars and associate with any men she damn well pleases? And while I'm at it, I could probably add, and choose her own clothes and her own hairdo and wear make-up if she wants to?"

Sam cut the head off of the mug of beer with his spatula and thought about it momentarily before shoving the brew over. He was a bartender of the old school, beefy, with large reddish hands, and came complete with white apron and bleary eyes.

He said, "Why, I don't know, Mr. Boleslaw. About eighteen, would you say?"

"Would you believe twenty-five?"

Sam obviously didn't know what he was talking about and so wiped the bar without noticeable achievement with his soiled bar rag.

He said, making conversation, "How goes the life of the john-fuzz these days, Mr. Boleslaw? Had any nice crimes lately?"

Tad looked at him in mock anger. "No, but if you use

that term again there's going to be one. And right here in this bar. And I'll be the one committing it.''

Sam leaned on the bar, after laughing appropriately. At this early time of the day, the only customer he had besides Tad was a tired-looking little man who sat in a booth nursing a highball. He had been nursing it for a long time and by the looks of him would continue to do so.

Sam said, ''What do you cops do, these days? Shucks, in my father's day they used to have bank robberies and the Mafia gangs shooting it out. All that sort of thing. Now we got the pseudo-dollar instead of paper money, and the National Data Banks and Universal Credit Cards, crime isn't practical any more. Nobody can spend somebody else's money, even if there was some way of getting it away from him.''

Tad finished his dark beer and motioned for a refill. While the bartender was drawing another, he said, ''Crime we will always have with us, Sam. It's just that the kind shifts around. Three or four hundred years ago they used to have highwaymen holding up stagecoaches. A hundred and fifty years ago they used to have types like Jesse and Frank James robbing trains. Nearly a hundred years ago characters like Dillinger and Bonnie and Clyde specialized on banks.''

''They all robbed money, or maybe jewelry and stuff like that,'' Sam insisted. ''But now we don't have no money.'' He cut the head off the fresh beer with his spatula and shoved it across to Tad, and resumed leaning on the bar.

Tad said, ''Well, eliminating money admittedly finished off a lot of crime, but there's still things such as crimes of passion. One of the patrol cars got a call the other night and when they got there they found a drunk so far gone that he didn't know what he had done. What he had done was crush his wife's head in with a baseball bat.''

Sam winced.

Tad said, after taking down a good quarter of the mug of beer, "Then there's the sex pervert."

"Homosexuality is legal now," Sam protested.

"Sure, between consenting adults and just so long as nobody is hurt. But some of these queers get a bit far out. Some don't go for adults, but for children instead. You'd be surprised how youthful children, sometimes. It'd turn your stomach. Or some get their jollies whipping or in other ways lousing up their sex partner. Last year we had to arrest a sadist on a homicide charge. He had literally whipped a girl to death." Tad took some more of the beer. "His defense was she liked it. She was a masochist."

"What's that?"

"Somebody who likes pain."

"Holy Jumping Zoroaster," Sam said. "But there's still no money to steal any more."

Tad said, "There's even angles to that. Narcotics, such as trank and soma, we still have with us. Kids, in particular, get hooked. We had a case just the other night. A stick-up romp. The citizen was armed and killed the boy first."

"But what could he get out of a stick-up, with no money any more?"

"Wrist chronometer, jewelry, expensive stylos, personal things like that. Things that just everybody carries around."

Sam was fascinated. "But what in the hell would the kid do with it?"

Tad finished the second beer and pushed the glass back.

"Flog them. The fence we will always have with us. Just a couple of days ago my buddy and I ran into a case where this character stole a two thousand pseudo-dollar diamond ring. He took it to a local shop and sold it to the dealer for three hundred pseudo-dollars. On that occasion we had been able to get a description of the diamond and soon located it." Tad didn't bother to tell the full Rex Moran story.

Sam was still fascinated, even as he drew the third beer. "What'd you do to the, uh, fence?"

Tad shook his head. "We couldn't do anything. He could claim he bought it in good faith. But we'll keep an eye on him and one of these days he'll outsmart himself, buying stolen goods."

Two more customers had entered and Sam had to go down and wait on them.

Tad was reasonably drenched when he left the bar a couple of hours later. He would have liked to have stayed, but his superiors took a dim view of any member of the police force being seen in public drenched. He still had in mind hanging a good one on, but he'd have to finish the process at home. He brought his Uni-Credit Card from his pocket and stuck it into the payment slot in the bar before him, then got off the stool and left.

XIII

Outside the bar, he brought forth his transeiver, flicked back the cover, activated it and summoned an autocab. The vacuum tube would have been cheaper and even faster, but he didn't want to be seen even partly under the weather and with his breath heavy with Sam's beer. The autocab zipped up to the curb and Tad got in and fumbled out his Uni-Credit Card, put it in the car's payment slot and dialed his apartment house, then returned the card to his pocket.

Using the card brought Rex Moran, or whatever his real name was, to mind. What a devil. Imagine figuring out that method of utilizing someone else's Universal Credit Card.

The autocab pulled up before the apartment building and the door opened automatically. Tad got out and entered the lobby and took an elevator. Before he could order his floor an elderly couple also got in.

She looked at Tad with distaste. Undoubtedly, she could smell his breath. Well, luckily he didn't know the couple. She looked the type who could have phoned in to headquarters and reported him drenched in public. Hell, he wasn't as far gone as all that. It was just that Sam served a brew rich in hops and as a result it packed a powerful bouquet.

He got out at his floor and made his way down the corridor to his mini-apartment. He shrugged out of his jacket, tossed it over the room's sole comfort chair, and went on over to his autobar. But no, the hell with ersatz guzzle, he reached up for a bottle of his diminishing stock of vodka. He didn't want to lose the edge he'd acquired at Sam's. He poured a healthy slug and carried it over to the couch.

He felt at loose ends. What was he going to do besides drink? He didn't feel much like reading and he didn't particularly go in for the Tri-Di shows. Most of them were based on violence of one type or the other and there was enough violence in his manner of making a living. Besides, they were such crap. Take Westerns. In the whole real history of the West, there wasn't a single case of Indians attacking a wagon train drawn up into a circle and riding around and around it while the pioneers picked them off wholesale. That wasn't the Indian way of fighting. They were guerrilla types and didn't believe in getting killed. They were more apt to run your horses off at night, or take a pot shot at you from ambush. Or take the war movies. The hero would invariably be an American, usually armed with a submachine gun. He'd fire hundreds of rounds from his twenty bullet clip, killing the bad guys —Germans, Japs, Reds— by the score. And whenever the bad guy took a hit he went down bang, dead as a duck. But whenever a good guy took a hit, he was either just wounded or had five minutes or more to get off his last words to his buddy, usually something involving sending a message to mother, or whoever. Crime shows, of course, were just burlesque to a professional cop.

No, the hell with Tri-Di. He considered going to the phone screen and getting one of the girls he usually dated to come over. One of those who liked a roll in the hay as much as he did.

Which one?

He didn't have to make the decision. The identity screen on the door buzzed.

Frowning, he activated it. Usually, he was at work this time of the evening and most of his acquaintances knew that. And his days off varied, so that if he wanted to get in touch with a friend, female or otherwise, he had to contact them.

He was really surprised when he saw that it was Tilly Brothers. Tilly Brothers! Coming to a man's apartment alone, and a single man's at that?

He hurried over to the door and let her in.

"Surprise, surprise," he said.

She hesitantly entered and looked about the tiny apartment.

She wasn't wearing her pink tinted glasses and as a result her blue eyes had that somewhat vague look worn by those who customarily do wear cheaters but have taken them off for whatever reason. She was also wearing both lipstick and eye make-up and her hair was done up in a less conservative style than he had seen her in before. But above all her dress wasn't so definitely one of yesteryear; in fact it was quite attractive, with almost a seductive quality.

She realized that he was taking her in and probably knew what he was thinking.

She flushed and said, in her small voice, "I realized that I was abrupt earlier in the day and thought I should apologize."

He was still flabbergasted but he managed to get out, "Not at all, Ms. Brothers. Not at all. Do have a chair."

He swept his jacket from the comfort chair, took it over to the closet and hung it up.

Even as she seated herself, he began to button his collar and to readjust his tie, which he had loosened earlier.

She said, "Oh, please remain comfortable."

He sat down on the couch, across from her and asked, "How in the world did you know where I lived?"

"You're in the phone book. I had a little trouble figuring out how you spelled your name. But finally I found it. There's only one other Boleslaw in the book and you're the only Tadeusz Boleslaw."

He shook his head. "I'm surprised that you took the trouble." He was still holding his glass of vodka in his hand. He said hurriedly, "But I'm being a terrible host. Could I offer you a drink? Oops. You don't drink. A soft drink, or coffee?"

She looked down at the tip of her shoe shyly and said, "When mother was still living with us, we sometimes had a sweet wine on Christmas or Thanksgiving or a birthday."

Sweet wine, yet. The drinker in Tad Boleslaw flinched, but he rose to the occasion, even as he came to his feet and headed for the autobar. He said, over his shoulder, "What kind do you prefer?"

She said, "I—I am afraid I don't know any of the names, Mr. Boleslaw."

"Tad," he told her. "And I'll call you Tilly. He reached up a hand for the sole bottle of wine in his private stock. "How would one of the heavier sherries do? Say, this Bristol Cream?"

"Heavier?" She looked hesitant.

"That means not dry. It has nothing to do with the strength. They're sweeter than the lighter sherries."

He took down a wine glass and poured before she said anything further. He carried it over to her.

She thanked him and sipped carefully and then looked up, smiled, and said, "Why, it's quite good."

"Surprisingly enough," he told her, resuming his seat, "guzzle doesn't have to taste bad." He took another sip of his vodka, and realized that maybe it didn't have to but often did. You drank vodka for the effect, not the taste.

She brought up her glass again and finished the sherry.

He blinked at her. "You're supposed to sip that stuff," he said. "It's not like taking a straight shot of whiskey or something."

She flushed furiously. "I—I'm sorry. I didn't know."

He came to his feet and smiled, and said, "Don't worry about it. I'll get you another, and you can practice sipping."

She looked as though she was about to protest, but didn't.

When he was reseated again, and they both were glass in hand—he had gotten a refill as well—he said, "You can't imagine how surprised I am to see you. Glad, of course, but, well, surprised."

She said, her voice more tiny than ever, "Father is at work at this time of night and I felt lonesome in the apartment alone."

"Oh? How did you know that I wasn't married?"

She looked down at the tip of her shoe again. "I looked you up on your Public Dossier in the National Data Banks."

He took her in for a long time. And she nervously nibbled at her drink as he did so. Evidently, even two glasses of sherry were enough to bring color to her cheeks.

He said finally, "Why did you really come, Tilly? Certainly not to apologize to a man that you haven't really been properly introduced to."

She looked at him quickly and said, "Don't you like me?"

"Of course, I like you. You're a very pretty girl and very sweet. And I'm a normal man. In fact, when it comes to pretty girls, I'm a bit more than normal."

"Well, don't other girls sometimes come to your apartment? I understand that bachelors . . . " She let the sentence dribble away.

He squinted at her quizzically, his head slightly tilted to one side. He said, "Why, yes, of course. But seldom, if ever, does one come here to apologize to me."

She finished her sherry and said, all but defiantly, "Well, why do they come?"

He decided to bring this to a head. The vodka, on top of Sam's beer, was working on him. He said flatly, "Usually to climb in bed with me."

Her easily come-by flush was there again, and her head was low. She said, her voice so small as hardly to be heard, "All right."

"*All right!* What do you mean, all right?" He couldn't have been more astonished if she had suddenly begun to do a striptease. "An inexperienced girl like you doesn't just come to a man's apartment and climb in bed with him."

She stood and said, "I'm not inexperienced. I've —been with men before."

He couldn't believe her. "You have?" he said. And then, suspiciously, "How many? Some high school seduction in the back of a car?"

She pursed her lips, defiantly. "Eight, altogether."

That stopped him.

She said, "Where is the bedroom?"

Tad sighed and said, "This is the bedroom."

He decided to call her bluff, got up and touched the button which unfolded the bed from the wall. He bent over it and pulled down the cover and looked at her.

She tightened her lips but then, "Turn your back," she said.

He turned his back and shortly could hear her undressing behind him.

Turn your back, yet! Modesty. He had a sneaking suspicion that she was lying, that she was still a virgin. But why?

She said, from the bed, "Aren't you going to turn out the light?"

"If you wish," he said.

He went over to the light switch and flicked it off, then undressed quickly and put his clothes on the couch. This was the most cold-blooded approach to the sex act he could offhand remember ever having participated in. On top of it all, on his way over to the light he had seen her in the bed, a sheet pulled up tight to her chin and her eyes wide.

Wide with fright? Should he call this off? But she was of age, certainly, and she had claimed to have had experiences with eight men. And, besides, she had been the aggressor. He shrugged and climbed into the bed beside her.

She was stiff. All but rigid. And her legs were tightly together.

He cupped one of her breasts in his right hand and she gasped. However, the nipple immediately began to go hard. He bent over her to kiss her and her mouth was tight, the lips hard as rock. It was like kissing his own mother.

Puzzled, he began stroking her body. She sucked in air. Her body was considerably nicer than he had expected. When he had first seen her, there in her father's apartment, he had thought her a trifle on the dumpy side. But that didn't project itself in bed. She had a lovely figure.

He bent to kiss her again, and her lips were as before. Completely unresponsive.

Tad sighed and threw back the covers and got up and went over to his clothes and began to re-dress. This was proving to be one hell of a day off, he decided. He couldn't even feel the guzzle any more.

"What's—what's the matter?" she said, complete lack of understanding in her voice.

"I'm evidently just not your type," he told her.

"But—but I like you fine—Tad."

"Like hell you do. Certainly not that way." Now dressed, he went back over to the light switch and flicked it on.

The sheet was up around her neck again.

He said wearily, "I'll turn my back. There's the bathroom over there. You get your clothes and take them in there and dress. I'm going to get myself another drink. I could use one."

He could hear her getting out of the bed, and then scurrying across the room. The bathroom door opened and closed.

Tad went over to where she had left her pocketbook and took it up and opened it. He took out her Universal Credit Card and memorized the number, then put it back. There was nothing else in the bag of any interest. He put it down again in the spot it had occupied before and went over to his bar and poured himself another vodka. He hadn't been exaggerating, he could use it. It was the damnedest experience he'd ever had with a girl. He snorted amusement. He must be losing his masculine charm.

He returned the bed to the wall and went over to the couch and resumed his seat there.

Shortly, she came out, looking the height of embarrassment. She looked down, toeing in, somewhat like a grammar school child up before the principal for some transgression.

"What did I do wrong?" she said lowly.

He growled, "You got into bed with me. That's what you did wrong."

He took a good pull at his drink and added, "Now, let's start all over again, Tilly. Why did you come here?"

It came out in a rush. "I thought I could persuade you, if I let you do what you wanted to me, to stop persecuting my father."

He stared at her. "Persecuting your father? Where in the world did you get that idea?"

"You've been checking on him, looking into his dossiers and all."

"Holy jumping Zoroaster, girl, that was just a routine check. After all, he has killed some men and under rather strange conditions."

"He was only defending himself!"

"That's what my superior told me. He pulled me off the case, so to speak. Currently, nobody, at least that I know of, is investigating your father."

She looked at him pleadingly. "Do you mean that?"

"Yes. How did you know I had been investigating him?"

"I—I can't tell you." She took up her bag. "Thank

you, oh, thank you—Tad,'' she said and hurried for the door.

He opened it for her and said, "You're a sweet girl, Tilly." Then sarcastically, "Are you sure it was eight?"

"Yes," she said, without turning her head, and started quickly down the corridor.

He looked after her for a long moment, then turned back into the apartment. He went over and got his glass and began to raise it to his lips. But then he abruptly put it down and went to his desk and dialed the National Data Banks on his screen.

He said, "I want the Dossier Complete of Tilly Brothers." He gave the number of her Universal Credit Card.

The screen said, "What is your classification, please? Are you eligible to request a citizen's Dossier Complete?"

"Police officer," he sighed and put his police I.D. card on the identification square of the screen.

And there was the life of Tilly Brothers.

It was rather routine, uneventful, even drab and color-less life, until a couple of years ago. He found what he was looking for under her medical record. She had been gang-raped by eight young hoodlums.

Tad flicked off the screen and stared at it for long moments.

His voice sick, he said aloud, "And you were going to make me number nine, you poor kid?"

XIV

When Tad Boleslaw arrived at headquarters the following day he was a bit early and Jim Kelly hadn't shown up as yet. There was a message for him to see Lieutenant Schmidt, so after he had gotten into uniform he went to Schmidt's office.

For once, the detective lieutenant wasn't working on his reports. Instead, he had his feet on his desk, his age-worn pipe in his mouth, and was gloomily watching three police report screens at once.

Tad said, "I got the message that you wanted to see me, Norm."

The lieutenant didn't bother to bring his feet down. He said, "It's the commissioner again. He wants you to come up."

Tad said, "What about?"

"It's good news—I think. But he wants to tell you himself. If you pull it off, it'll probably lead to a promotion."

"Wizard," Tad blurted. He turned to go, but then reversed himself and said, "A funny thing happened yesterday, Norm. I ran into the daughter of Charles Brothers."

Schmidt looked at him. "I thought I told you to lay off Brothers."

"It was an accidental meeting."

"Well, what's funny about it?"

"She—uh, pleaded with me to stop persecuting her father. She seemed to know that I had dug into his dossiers." Tad slipped in a quick fib at this point. "Back before you told me to drop it. How in the name of Zoroaster could she have known?"

Schmidt thought about it, scowling. "Damned if I know, Tad. But it's not important. Just lay off the guy. Go on up and see the commissioner."

"Doesn't he want Jim, too?"

"It would seem not."

Tad made his way to the elevators and shortly was in the reception room of the police commissioner's office. The same sergeant, as before, was behind the desk there. As before, he gestured at the door leading to the inner office with a thumb. Tad didn't know the receptionist sergeant. He wondered if he could talk.

He entered and was surprised to find that Warren Hammond was again present.

Commissioner Marvin Ruhling beamed at him and said, "Good evening, ah, Tad is your nickname, isn't it? Sit down, my boy."

Tad nodded at Hammond and received a friendly nod in return, and found a straight chair and sat down.

Ruhling said, "We'll come straight to the point. Mr. Hammond has stayed on in Center City for a couple of days, Tad, and we've discussed the desirability of using our fair town for further investigation into criminal methods of subverting the Universal Credit Card. Do you wish to take over, Mr. Hammond?"

"Yes, of course." The National Data Bank big shot looked at Tad. "In spite of the fact that you were unable to apprehend Rex Moran in the twenty-four hour period he had at his command, I was impressed by your aptitude, Patrolman Boleslaw.''

"Thank you, sir. But, as you say, Jim and I flunked it.''

"Rex Moran is my top field man. And you were working in the dark. However, you located the diamond ring almost immediately and were able to get a fix on him in that autocafeteria. Hadn't it been for your praiseworthy desire to avoid a shoot-out in a crowded public place, you would have nabbed him then and there and he would have lost the wager. But you, of course, had no way of knowing that Rex would not have used his gun.''

"Yes, sir.''

The older man went on, whilst Commissioner Ruhling continued to beam. Tad was beginning to suspect that his ultimate superior's job was a political plum and that the commissioner wasn't particularly smart. But that's the way things went these days—and any days.

Hammond said, "We've come up with a plan to organize a present day equivalent of a Bunco Squad.''

That was a new one to Tad Boleslaw. He said, "Bunco Squad?''

"A term used in the old days when there were still a good many confidence men in the criminal elements. The Bunco Squad dealt with them. Supposedly, the day of the confidence man has ended, however, there would seem to be a revival, on a different level. Today, the equivalent of the con man now deals primarily through the National Data Banks and particularly the banking section of them.

"At any rate, you and your partner, Patrolman Kelly, are to be our embryonic Bunco Squad here in Center City. If the plan works out, undoubtedly we will inaugurate similar police elements in all areas of the nation.''

So this was the good news with possible promotion that Norm Schmidt was talking about. Tad glowed inwardly. This was the big chance he had been waiting for.

Hammond said, "I will be expecting continuing reports from you to my offices in New Denver. You will be in charge of our miniature Bunco Squad."

Tad hesitated before saying, "But, sir, Jim Kelly has ten years of seniority on me."

"But still remains a patrolman," the commissioner put in. "We checked thoroughly both of your records, Tad. And were more largely impressed by yours. I am afraid that Jim Kelly is a bit on the stolid and uninspired side."

"He taught me everything I know, sir."

The commissioner smiled, and said, "Are you arguing with me, Tad?"

"No, sir." He looked at the National Data Banks man. "Just what in particular are we looking for, Mr. Hammond?"

The other shrugged. "I wouldn't know. That's your job. You are to locate and to apprehend these sharpies that are getting around our section. We don't even know how many successful ones there are. Obviously, those who are successful aren't caught. From time to time we have been able to arrest some of the more stupid but your job is to seek out the more astute ones who thus far have remained free and feed upon the rest of society."

"Yes, sir." Inwardly, Tad Boleslaw felt dismay. *This* was his big chance? He didn't have the vaguest idea where to begin. He said, "Are there any inklings at all, a point from which I could begin?"

The question wasn't very well received by either of the others. What had they expected him to do, dash out the door and begin arresting mishandlers of the Universal Credit Card right and left?

Hammond said, ''We will forward to you complete reports on cases we have successfully handled through my section. As I told you, these are mostly picayunish operators.''

''What would be an example, sir?'' Tad said, feeling a little desperate.

Hammond thought a moment before saying, ''For instance, we have had several cases of small time blackmailers. They would get something—anything—on another citizen then force him to buy things with his Universal Credit Card and turn them over. On the face of it, this can't be too big an operation. The largest I know of was a blackmailer who discovered an affair a supposedly happily married man was conducting with a young woman, who turned out, eventually, to be an accomplice of the criminal. He forced his victim to buy him a sports aircraft, of all things. He was revealed because it was obvious he didn't have the wherewithal to purchase such a craft. Most of the blackmailers are less ambitious. They get wrist chronometers, jewelry, furniture, clothes and such items. The smaller the items, the more difficult to find the transgressor.''

''Yes, sir, I can see that.''

The commissioner rubbed his hands together and said happily, ''Well, there you are, Tad, my boy. All the best of luck.''

''Yes, sir,'' Tad said gloomily, coming to his feet at the dismissal.

Hammond waggled a finger at him. ''And remember, I want continuing reports on your progress. I believe that I shall assign Rex Moran to handle the matter from our end in New Denver.''

Continuing reports, yet. And that sharpy Rex Moran goosing him along. Holy jumping Zoroaster.

''I'll get right at it, gentlemen,'' Tad said and headed for the door.

He went back to Schmidt's office and found Jim Kelly there, along with the lieutenant.

His usually sour superior was grinning. ''What'd I tell you?'' he said.

Tad grunted at him. ''You told me it was good news.''

Kelly said, looking from one of them to the other, ''What goes on?''

Tad said to him, ''We're the new Bunco Squad.'' And then to Norm Schmidt, ''What the hell are you grinning about? Sherlock Holmes couldn't make headway on this one.''

''Who's Surelock Homes?'' Kelly said.

Schmidt said, ''Pull this off, Tad, and you'll only be a detective sergeant for beginners.''

''Yeah. And if I don't pull it off I suspect I'll be a patrolman until retirement—if I'm not fired.''

Kelly said, ''What goes on?''

Tad said, ''Come on, Jim. Let's go get a drink and I'll tell you about it.''

''Get a drink? We're already overdue to go on patrol, Tad.''

''We already *are* on patrol,'' Tad told him. ''But this time it's a different kind of patrol. Our new job is to find and outsmart funkers who are smarter than we are.''

They crossed the street to the nearest tavern, which was across the street from headquarters. Like The Hole, Sam's place, down in The Mall, it was one of the few in Center City that still boasted a live bartender. They took stools at the bar.

Harry came down to them, drying his chubby hands on his less than spotless apron and frowning. He said, "You boys are in uniform. You sure you want a drink?"

Jim said, "Make mine a Del Valle, instead, Harry."

Tad said, "The hell with that. Give us a couple of double tequilas."

Both Harry and Jim stared at him.

Tad said, "From now on, we're actually under nobody's orders but our own. We make up our own rules."

The bartender shrugged and began getting the drinks together. He said, "Don't blame me if a sergeant or lieutenant on his day off comes in and spots you."

Harry cut a lime into four quarters, brought out a shaker of salt, then poured two king-size shots of white tequila.

Tad took his up and headed for a booth. Jim shrugged and followed.

In the booth, they went through the routine. You sprinkled some of the salt on the back of your hand, licked it, took up the tequila and knocked it back over your tonsils, then grabbed up the lime and bit into it before your throat was seared.

"Holy jumping Zoroaster," Jim protested, "but that's strong." He looked at Tad accusingly. "Now what goes on?"

Tad told him the whole story.

Jim slumped back in his seat. "Wow," he said.

Tad was embarrassed. "Jim," he said, "they've made me chief of the so-called squad."

"Wizard," his buddy told him. "That makes sense."

"But you're the most experienced man on the team."

Jim Kelly grinned at him. "Me and Molly decided a long time ago, Tad, that I wasn't going to make it no further. I'm due for retirement in five years. But you're like a son to me, and I been bucking for you all along."

"Thanks, Jim," Tad said in relief. "But where do we start? Like I said, these funkers that Hammond wants us to catch are smarter than we are, or they wouldn't be getting away with it."

"We'll see about that," Jim said, bending his face into unwonted thought. He signaled Harry for another round.

Harry called over unbelievingly, "You mean another double? Aren't you guys supposed to be on patrol?"

"Shut up," Tad called back.

Jim said, "You know where we ought to start?"

"No, damn it."

"Checking out funkers who are on their Inalienable Basic income and are living higher on the hog than it calls for. We oughta be able to get that information out of the data banks. First we find out who they are, then we gotta figure out how they're doing it."

Tad stared at him. "You're right," he said. "Hell, it couldn't be simpler. If Rex Moran can't supply that kind of information for us, what the hell can he do?" He added, "You know, maybe you should have been the head man in this Bunco Squad at that."

"No thanks," Jim said. "How in the blithering devil did this Inalienable Basic, Universal Credit Cards and all the rest of it get started, anyway?"

"I suppose it was inevitable," Tad said thoughtfully. "We were heading for it from several different directions but didn't know it. It started with money. Originally money was usually gold or silver. But even gold is too heavy and awkward to carry around easily in any large amounts, so governments started issuing paper money, backed by gold or silver. Any time you wanted to you could take your paper money to a bank and redeem it. But after a few king-size wars and depressions, and all-out spending for defense, and the space program, the government of the United States in particular began running big deficits in spending, what with the national budget being over 300 billion a year. So they printed up more money than they had backing for. After a while they'd printed up over fifty billion dollars, with practically no gold to back it. So they discontinued paying off at all. It was galloping inflation and the country was facing total collapse. As a matter of fact, practically all other countries were doing the same and after awhile there wasn't enough gold in the world to begin to back all the currency.''

"What the hell's all that got to do with Inalienable Basic?'' Jim said, sipping gingerly at the new tequila which Harry had brought them.

"They had to find a new backing for their money, so the government had the top 200 corporations of the country pay ten percent of their taxes in the form of their common stock. They amalgamated this into what amounted to a gigantic mutual fund called United States Basic Common and put it on every stock exchange in the world to seek its level. And then they announced that anybody who wanted to redeem their dollars would be paid off in this stock. Obviously it was valuable stuff and paid good dividends.''

"But what's that got to do . . . ''

Tad overrode him. "It worked fine. Our money was

backed by a trillion dollar a year economy. So next year the government did it again. Meanwhile, relief, pensions, and so forth were in a mess and getting worse, what with the unemployment growing with automation and computerization. So the government began issuing what they called Inalienable Basic in the way of old age pensions, relief for the unemployable and so forth. Recipients got their dividends from this, but couldn't sell the stock and it reverted to the government upon death. As time went by, more and more people became eligible and finally the government decided to end poverty once and for all by issuing everybody ten shares.

"At the same time, computer data banks had been growing geometrically and finally they were merged into the National Data Banks. And at the same time the use of credit cards was growing fabulously. And at the same time crime was growing like crazy. They solved, or nearly solved, all three problems by creating the Universal Credit Card and the pseudo-dollar and the old paper money was slowly redeemed, even that which was abroad."

"How about Variable Basic?" Jim said, finishing his drink.

"Well, as the amount of United States Basic Common stock increased, more and more of it was bought by investors. This *could* be bought and sold by those who could afford it, so it came to be known as Variable Basic. And that's where we are now. Poverty has been done away with, inflation eliminated, and crime is largely impractical since there is no money to steal. We've still got the old stock markets and so forth but it's getting to the point where so much of the country's stock is in the government's hands that they're beginning to call it People's Capitalism. Hell, didn't you learn all this in school?''

''If I did, I forgot most of it. School never was my strong point. Have you got any shares of Variable Basic, Tad?''

''Five shares. How about you?''

Jim said proudly, ''Me and Molly have thirty-six. You see, what with my police pay, and four of us in the family with our Inalienable Basic income, we can live pretty good and still save for the time I retire and the kids are grown.''

''Not bad,'' Tad said, coming to his feet. ''Let's get going. We're going to have to start checking out funkers in Center City who are living beyond their income.''

XV

Jim was at the controls. He said, "Well, who's the first one?"

Tad looked down at the notebook in his hand. "Phidias Porras, alias Rosy Porras. No income beyond his Inalienable Basic dividends and he seems to live like a millionaire. No job and he doesn't own any Variable Basic."

"I don't remember him," Jim said. "Was there anything in his Crime Dossier?"

"Nothing much. Largely routine. He's alleged to sometimes carry a shooter, but he's never been caught with it. It's probably like Hammond said. The really smart ones don't get caught. Of course, we don't know what his racket is and if it involves jimmying the National Data Banks. For all we know, he's a great lover with a lot of rich girls and they buy him everything he wants."

"That sounds like the life," Jim said.

Tad looked over at him, pretending surprise. "And you a happily married man?"

Jim grinned. "I can dream, can't I? Hey, there's the apartment building. He lives in a pretty swank pad for a funker with nothing but ten shares of Inalienable Basic."

The patrol car swooped in to a landing.

Rosy Porras shucked off his jacket and began to shrug into the holster harness. As he settled it around his chest, he scowled at the row of sports jackets in his closet. Styles, these days, weren't conducive to concealing a heavy-calibered shooter.

A bell tinkled and Rosy turned his scowl to the screen sitting next to the bed. He wasn't expecting anybody. He hesitated a moment, unbuckled the harness again and threw it into a chair, then went over and flicked on the door screen switch.

It was a stranger, and he wore a police cap. He was young and efficient looking, his face expressionless.

Rosy pursed his lips in surprise.

Well, there was no putting it off. He reversed the switch so that the policeman could see him as well and said, "Yeah?"

The stranger said, "Phidias Porras?"

Rosy winced at the use of his real name. It had been some time since he had been exposed to it. He growled, "What do you want?"

The other said, "I'm Patrolman Tad Boleslaw. Bunco Squad of the Center City Police, working in conjunction with the National Data Banks. I'd like to talk to you, Citizen."

Rosy Porras scowled at him. A police snooper. That's all he needed right now, with the boys expecting him in a few minutes.

"About what?" Rosy said. "Listen, I'm busy."

The other looked at him patiently and said, "About your sources of income, Citizen."

Rosy said, "That's none of your business."

Tad Boleslaw said, still patiently, "To the contrary, Citizen Porras, it's my job."

"You got a warrant?"

107

Patrolman Boleslaw said slowly, "Do you really want me to get one, or can we just sit down and have a chat?"

"Wait a minute," Porras growled in disgust. He flicked off the screen, bent over and picked up the shooter and holster. He put them in a drawer and locked it and then left the bedroom and went on through the living room to the apartment's front door. He opened it and let the patrolman in. He was followed by another cop.

Tad said, "This is Patrolman Jim Kelly."

He stepped suddenly forward toward Rosy Porras and patted him here, there—a quick frisking.

Rosy Porras stepped back in indignation, snarling, "Hey, take it easy, you flat. What kind of curd you pulling off?"

Tad said mildly, "It's been reported that you sometimes go heeled, even in this day and age, Phidias."

Porras winced again. "Listen, call me Rosy," he growled. "Everybody does." He led the way into the living room.

Tad Boleslaw let his eyes go around the room and did a silent whistle of appreciation. "No wonder they call you Rosy, in view of the fact that we haven't been able to find in your Dossier Complete any record of you working since you came of age. Things are pretty rosy, aren't they? How do you manage to maintain this apartment on the credit income from your Inalienable Basic? It doesn't begin to call for a place like this."

Rosy had started for the autobar but, remembering what the evening had in prospect, changed his mind and sank down into a chair. He didn't invite the others to be seated.

He said, "A friend loans it to me."

"I see. Where is this friend?"

"He's on a vacation over in Common Europe."

"And when will he be back?"

"I don't know," Porras said defiantly. "It's a long vacation. Listen, what business is it of yours?"

"Sounds like a pretty good friend," Jim muttered.

Tad Boleslaw had taken a place on a couch. He looked about the room again. "And all these rather expensive furnishings. They belong to your friend too?"

"Some of them," Rosy said. "And some of them are mine."

Tad brought a notebook from his tunic pocket and flicked through it, coming to the page he wanted. "Phidias Porras. Registered for employment in Category Baking, Sub-Division Pretzel Bender." He frowned. "What in the name of Zoroaster is a pretzel bender?"

Rosy Porras flushed. "How'd I know? I was more or less born into the category. My old man was a pretzel bender and his old man. So I registered for it when I came of employable age. But that branch of baking got automated out of existence a long time ago. Can I help it if there is no such work? I just live on my credits from Inalienable Basic."

Kelly looked at him patiently. "You drive a late model hovercar. Where did you get the credits for it?"

"I won it gambling."

"Oh, come on now," Tad said.

Rosy Porras, in exaggerated nonchalance, crossed one leg over the other. He said reasonably, "There's no regulation against gambling."

Tad said in disgust, "Don't be ridiculous. Gambling isn't practical on anything but a matchstick level. Of course, there's no law against it, but when our system of exchange is such that no one but you, yourself, can spend the credits you acquire as dividends on your Inalienable Basic, or whatever you earn above your basic dividends, gambling becomes nonsense. Why, you can't even transfer pseudo-dollars from one account to another unless you're a licensed businessman.''

Porras was shaking his head at him. ''Now that's where your National Data Banks people haven't figured out this fancy system to its end. Stutes who like to gamble, like to gamble period, and they'll find a way, and not for matchsticks. Sure, we can't spend each other's credits but we can gamble for *things*. Suppose a dozen or so poker addicts form kind of a club. One of them sticks in his hovercar which he had to pony up several thousand pseudo-dollars for. Another puts in a fancy camera that he had to pay a couple of hundred pseudo-dollars for. Another one, an expensive wrist chronometer. Okay, wizard. The banker issues chips for the credit value of every item the group members put up. And if any member wins enough credit chips he can 'buy' the thing he wants out of the club kitty.''

Kelly said, ''I'll be damned.''

Rosy Porras snorted amusement. ''You mean you two never heard of gambling clubs?''

Tad Boleslaw cleared his throat. He said, ruefully, ''Undoubtedly, we'll be hearing more about them soon. There's no regulation against them now, but there should be.''

''Why?'' Porras said, letting his voice go plaintive. ''Listen, why can't you john-fuzz characters leave off fouling up everybody you can?''

The patrolman said patiently, "Because under People's Capitalism, Citizen, no one can steal, cheat or con anybody else out of his means of exchange. Or, at least, that's why our Bunco Squad exists. The National Data Banks people are interested in how a Rosy Porras can live extremely well without having performed any useful contribution in any field for his whole adult life."

Rosy's expression made it clear that he was being imposed upon. "Listen," he said. "I got a lot of friends. I haven't been too well lately. I been sick, see? Okay, so these friends of mine pick up the tab here and there."

"You mean friends have been discharging your obligations by using their credits to pay your bills?"

"There's no regulation against it."

"No, there isn't," Tad said unhappily. "But discharging a grocery bill in an ultra-market isn't exactly the sort of gift one gives a man in his prime."

"No regulation against it," Porras insisted.

Tad said, "And this is your sole method of income, save your dividends from your Inalienable Basic stock?"

"I didn't say that. I do a lot of people a lot of favors and then maybe they do me one. And, like I said, I belong to some of these gambling clubs."

"And always win?"

Rosy shrugged hugely. "They don't call me Rosy for nothing. I'm pretty lucky. Listen, I got some business needs taking care of. Do you really have anything on me, or are you just wasting both our time?"

Tad Boleslaw came to his feet with a sigh. He looked down into his notebook again. "General Aptitude I.Q. 136," he read. He looked up at Porras. "And here you are, a full-time bum."

Rosy stood too, scowling. "Listen," he said, "I don't have to take that from you. You got my category. I'm a pretzel bender by trade. What can I do? The job's been automated out of existence."

"You can always switch categories. Study up on some new one. With an I.Q. like yours, you wouldn't have much trouble getting a job."

Rosy sneered. "Sure, that's the theory. And maybe it sounds good to somebody like you who's got a job. Your old man was probably john-fuzz too and got you into police school. That's the way it works. I'm not stupid. In this day and age, there just aren't hardly any jobs."

Tad looked at him speculatively. "We'll see just how stupid and phony you are, Porras. I have a sneaking suspicion that you're going to wind up in a Psychotherapy Institute, Citizen."

"Yeah? Listen, my little chum-pal, I got a lot of friends, understand. You'll have your work cut out getting me into a pressure cooker."

"We'll see about that," Jim Kelly said grimly. Tad was already on his way to the door. Kelly followed, adding over his shoulder. "And we'll see you later, Rosy."

Rosy Porras scowled after them. It didn't do a man any good to have the john-fuzz on his tail. He wondered uncomfortably what he had done to draw their attention. In this age, a grifter's first need was to remain inconspicuous.

He turned and went back to the drawer where he had locked up his gun and harness.

XVI

High above, Tad Boleslaw was concentrating on the binocular screen of their patrol helio-jet.

He said to Jim, "There he goes. Do you make him? He's climbing into that hovercar. The license number on the roof is 120-1516."

"I got him," Jim said. "But he's going to figure on the possibility of a police patrol being on him."

"That's okay," Tad said comfortably. "You know, I've got the feeling that whatever it is he does, he's going to do it tonight."

"Going mystical on me again, eh?" Jim said. "Next you'll be reading palms."

Rosy Porras was already late but he was taking no chances. He drove his hovercar into the downtown area and into the heaviest traffic and then spent the next twenty minutes doubling and doubling back still again. All he needed was for some snooper such as Boleslaw to be shadowing him.

Evidently, he was clear. He finally left the car in the parking cellars of a large hotel and made his way to one of the popular autobars above. He found an empty booth and dialed a drink, putting his credit card into the table's slot. This was one of the few things he had to use his own skimpy pseudo-dollars for. He sipped the drink slowly and checked the occupants of the other tables unobtrusively.

When he was convinced of their innocence, he let his finger thump twice on the table and Pop Rasch and Martin Zogbaum came over and sat down with him.

Pop Rasch, a heavy-set, gray-faced man with obvious false teeth, said angrily, "Where in the name of holy Zoroaster you been? We were about to fold the whole job."

Rosy Porras said, "A snooper from the police turned up and grilled me at the apartment.

Pop said, "Oh, oh."

Porras waved a hand negligently, negatively. "It was nothing, just routine. Wanted to know how I managed to live so well on nothing but Inalienable Basic." He laughed.

"How'd he know where to find you?" Pop said uneasily.

"I suppose they got ways. Anyway, I guess I'd better move on. We been working this town too hard anyway. Maybe I'll go out to the West Coast."

Martin Zogbaum, a clerkish-looking type and out of place with these two, said nervously, "Well, I suppose then that we'd better call off tonight's, ah, romp."

"Romp," Rosy snorted at him. "You been watching those Tri-Di detective shows?" His tone held deprecation.

Zogbaum said defensively, "I'll watch whatever I please, Porras."

"Okay, wizard," Pop Rasch said. "Let's not get into a silly argument. That's just what we need right in the middle of a job. In the old days, they used to call a romp a caper. But the hell with it. What'd you say, Rosy? Should we call it all off?"

Rosy Porras grumbled, "Can't afford to now. We need a good taw in case of emergencies."

Martin Zogbaum said, still miffed, "Maybe you do, but I work in my category. I've got a job and I'm clean."

Rosy snorted. "You're about as clean as a mud pack. You put in minimum time on that job of yours and live like some of these upperclass who hold down premium jobs. The first time this new Bunco Squad gets around to checking you, you're going to be doing some fast talking."

Pop Rasch said, "And all we have to do is start squabbling among ourselves and we'll all wind up in a Category Medicine Psychotherapy Institute, learning to adjust to society." He grimaced at the thought.

Rosy said, "Listen, let's get going. We've been casing the job for weeks. There's no point in panicking out now. Nothing's happened except that a john-fuzz snooper named Boleslaw talked to me for about fifteen minutes."

"Boleslaw," Pop Rasch said.

Rosy looked at him. "Somebody you know?"

Rasch said thoughtfully, "Yeah. And I knew his father before him. Good cops—if there is anything as good john-fuzz. One of these yokes who takes his work seriously. Tough, but fair. I got a friend who ran into this Boleslaw."

Zogbaum blinked nervously, "What happened to him?"

"What'd ya think happened to him? He's got a silly job now stooging for some Category Research double-dome or something. Why, when I see him on the street, he's hard put to remember me. Brainwashed."

Rosy Porras got to his feet and growled, "Let's get going. It's late enough as it is."

They took Pop Rasch's heavy sedan to the records section of the Administration Building which they had already cased thoroughly. They parked half a block down from a side entry. Pop Rasch and Martin Zogbaum sat in the front seat, Rosy in the back.

Rosy opened the overnight bag which Rasch and Zogbaum had brought along and unfolded a long, pipe-like device. He screwed an object resembling a wind instrument's mouthpiece to the end.

He said, "You're sure of these details, eh?"

"Yes, yes," Zogbaum said nervously. "He's the only one in the building at night. He sets up various routine matters for the day shift. But for all I know, he's already gone in. I think we're late. Perhaps we'd better put it off."

"Don't be a funker," Rosy growled.

"Here comes somebody now," Pop Rasch whispered.

"It's him," Zogbaum whispered back. "Are you sure that we shouldn't . . . "

"Knock it," Rosy said.

The lone pedestrian passed without looking at them. When he had gone a dozen feet or so, Rosy Porras rested his pipe on the ledge of the window and puffed a heavy breath of air into the mouthpiece.

The pedestrian clapped a hand to his neck as though swatting a mosquito, and went on.

Rosy grinned. He began taking his device apart again. "There's the world for you," he told his companions. "The simpler thing you use, the bigger the wrench you can throw into the most complicated machinery these double-domes can dream up. A blowgun!"

Pop Rasch said, "This was your idea, Rosy. How soon will it hit him?"

"In about fifteen minutes. Then he'll go out like a light and wake up in maybe six hours with a blockbuster headache but no memory of anything but sleeping."

"That'll give us plenty of time to finish the, uh," —Zogbaum looked at Rosy defiantly, " —romp and leave the place all cleaned up so that nobody'll ever know we've been there. Six hours is plenty of time."

Pop Rasch looked at him. "Why don't you take a trank?" he said. "Nothing to be nervous about. All we gotta do is sit here for twenty minutes."

"I can't afford to be tranked," Zogbaum said. "I've got to be able to concentrate. And I hate to wait."

At the end of the twenty minutes they left the car and walked unhurriedly to the door of the building which the lone pedestrian had entered. The street was deserted at this time of night. Pop Rasch carried the valise.

Pop looked up and down the street as a double check, then hunkered down, while Rosy acted as watchman. The lock on the door yielded to his efforts in a matter of moments.

Pop Rasch sighed and said, "They don't make them the way they used to. No challenge, like." He added, a note of nostalgia in his voice, "They don't even have no watchmen anymore. In the old days, you had to take the watchman, some way or other."

Rosy Porras entered first. He looked up and down the halls. Some lights were burning. Not many. The Administration Building was inoperative at night.

"All clear," he said. "Let's go." Automatically, he shrugged his shoulders to loosen his harness and have the feel of the handgun ready to be drawn.

They proceeded down the hall. Pop Rasch had a simple chart of the building in his hand. They turned several corners, finally emerged into a long room banked with tabulaters, collators, sorters and computers. Leading off it, in turn, were several rooms of punched card files, and especially tape files, and shelves of bound reports.

"Wizard," Pop said to Zogbaum. "Now you're the boss. Go to it. Just for luck, I'm going to look up that cloddy Rosy claims is going to be sleeping for the rest of the night."

"It's not necessary," Rosy growled. "He's got enough dope to keep him under. All he's got to worry about is how to explain to his boss that he didn't do his routine work tonight."

"Just the same," Pop said, "double checking never hurt nobody—especially since he's the only guy in the building."

Martin Zogbaum wet his lips nervously and entered the first of the file rooms, after taking up the valise. He opened the bag and brought forth a sheaf of closely typed reports.

He said importantly, "Now you two leave me alone. I have to concentrate." He fished from the valise a small manually-operated card punch and some other equipment.

"Take it easy, fella," Rosy said tolerantly. "You're on your own. Don't worry about anything. I'm the heavy. I'll stand guard."

Pop Rasch left on his checking mission.

Zogbaum looked after him and said, "Do you think anything could have actually happened? I mean about that man actually not being unconscious?"

Rosy yawned. "No. Pop's just an old hand. He checks everything out. That's why he's lasted this long without winding up in some Psychotherapy Institute. And that's why I'm teamed up with him. With Pop and me on your side, you're like you're in your mother's arms, kid."

Martin Zogbaum snorted, but turned to his work.

Tad and Jim Kelly swooped in, both of them looking puzzled.

They parked beneath the dark of a tree and stared at the Administration Building.

"Why in the hell would they want to go in there?" Jim said.

"Damned if I know," Tad said. "Did you make either of the other two, besides Porras?"

"I didn't have much chance, and we were pretty high so that they wouldn't spot us. Besides, this night binocular gismo isn't as efficient as it might be. However, I think one of them was Pop Rasch."

"Never heard of him."

"Old, old-timer. Got a sizable Crime Dossier but he's never taken a real fall. Not one big enough to be psyched. Lot of petty stuff. If he's pulled any big romps, they never caught him."

Tad said, "Well, whatever they're up to, it's illegal. He obviously picked the lock on that door. That was clear enough in the binocular screen."

He flicked on the communication screen and said to the sergeant on the desk, "This is Kelly and Boleslaw, Bunco Squad. Send in three patrol cars." He gave the coordinates. "Have them come in quietly. We've got to surround a building. Three suspects inside, one of them is reputed to sometimes carry a shooter."

"Got you," the sergeant said.

XVII

Rosy Porras had remained free to operate on the wrong side of a society that was supposedly crime-free only by exercising an instinct for self-preservation that had served him well on more than one occasion when he found himself in the dill.

Something didn't feel right now.

Pop Rasch, the old pro, capable of becoming bored even while on a job, had sunk into a swivel chair and had actually drifted off into a fitful sleep, snoring raspingly.

Martin Zogbaum was busy in the files, humming and sometimes whistling to himself in concentration. He'd pull a card here, another there, sometimes substituting one from the valise, sometimes punching another hole or so. On several occasions, he displaced whole boxes of tapes, or cards, and actually stored three of them away in the bag.

Rosy Porras, suddenly unhappy without knowing why, left the room and retraced the route by which they had progressed through the building. Something was gnawing at him.

He returned to the door by which they had entered and opened it a fraction to peer out along the darkened street. In moments, his eyes had accustomed themselves to the lesser light.

There were three hovercars that hadn't been present earlier, parked out there, halfway down the street.

He closed the door quickly. His face was expressionless. The gun slid into his hand as though magically commanded. He stood for a moment in thought, then moved in quick decision.

He paralleled the wall for several hundred feet, along the semidark hallway, then stopped by a window. Again it took a while for his eyes to accustom themselves to the dark outside. Across the street were a small park, trees, bushes, a small fountain.

There was a man quietly sitting on a bench alone. After a time Rosy Porras was able to make out two other figures standing behind tree trunks.

There was no doubt about how things stood now. The whole thing had pickled. Rosy moistened dry lips. He hurried back to the room where Martin Zogbaum still labored over the punched cards and the tape files. Pop Rasch still slumbered fitfully.

Rosy fumbled through the report sheets which Zogbaum had brought with him. He kept his voice even. "You finished with this one of Dave Shriner?" he said.

Zogbaum looked up impatiently. "Shriner, Shriner? I don't remember them by name."

Rosy said, "Code 22D-11411-88M."

"Oh, that one. Yes," Zogbaum muttered. "All finished with that. Don't bother me now. I've got a dozen to go."

"Okay," Rosy said. Unobtrusively, he put the report sheet in his pocket and left the room.

He walked softly past Pop Rasch and made his way back into the corridor. He set off at a pace for the far side of the large building, making his way by instinct and quick animal reasoning rather than by knowledge of this part of the establishment.

Up one corridor and down another.

It was a matter of ditching the other two. Pop Rasch was too old to move fast enough and Zogoaum was too jittery in the dill to trust. The situation had pickled now and it was each man for himself.

He came finally to a window that opened on a dark alley-like entryway. He peered through it and could see nothing. He flicked the window's simple lock and drew it aside. He threw a leg over the sill and dropped to the ground below.

A voice that he recognized as that of Tad Boleslaw, chuckled and said, "Got you, you funker!" Rosy Porras felt arms go around his body.

He dropped suddenly, letting his legs go from under him so that the full weight of his body was on the other's arms. He fell on through, his buttocks hitting the ground. Without aim, he threw a pile-driving punch upward and struck low into Boleslaw's stomach.

Tad Boleslaw's voice which had chuckled but a moment before, gave out with a deep groan of anguish. Rosy rolled quickly, came to his feet and lashed out at him with both hands. It was too dark to strike accurately but he could tell that Boleslaw had crumpled.

The gun was in his hand again and he peered down indecisively. He had no time to make sure of Boleslaw. He spun quickly and ran for the entryway.

He paused a moment there and looked out. The way seemed clear. This part of the Administration Building opened onto the back of extensive offices, devoted to lower echelon workers. He holstered the gun.

XVIII

Rosy Porras walked rapidly but kept himself from a run. It was a matter now of relying on the good fortune his name promised. It was a matter of getting to a hovercab before things exploded behind him.

But even as he hurried toward a more traffic-ridden street, his mind was checking back, re-evaluating. Whatever had gone wrong, shouldn't have. It was all but impossible. Neither Zogbaum, nor certainly Pop Rasch, would have purposely betrayed them. Not any way that he could figure it.

He went back over the day. There had been nothing untoward until the appearance of those two patrolmen. Could he have said anything to that Boleslaw that had given the other a clue? No. Was there any manner in which Boleslaw and his partner could have tailed him? No. He had taken every precaution and then, after he had met the others, they had once again made sure that they were not being followed.

He reached an entertainment area and hurried to a cab park. He began to dial the coordinates of his apartment but then brought himself up sharp. He dialed the address of a hotel nearby instead.

He leaned back in the hovercab and forced his mind along the path of the past few days. No, there was nothing until Boleslaw and Kelly had shown up. His lips thinned in a grimace of rage. The cool efficiency of the damned snooper. The way he'd calmly entered the Porras apartment and then had the nerve to run his hands over Rosy's body, checking for a gun. The frisking!

That was it! Rosy Porras quickly ran his hands through his pockets, the pockets Tad Boleslaw had touched. He found it nestled down beneath a key ring and a cigarette lighter. A tiny device, no bigger than a shirt button.

Rosy stared at it and snarled. He threw it out into the street. A sub-miniature direction transmitter! Boleslaw had planted it on him back there in the apartment and the two cops had then been able to tail him at their leisure. A trick as simple as that. Pop Rasch would have laughed him to scorn.

They probably had Pop by now and Zogbaum, too. And here he was on the run, simply because he'd been too stupid to consider the possibility of his having a bug planted on him. He left the hovercab at the hotel near his apartment, making a mental note of the fact that he must not use his credit card again. Undoubtedly, that smart-assed Boleslaw would notify the National Data Banks to get a fix on his location, any time he used it.

He walked through the lobby, passing by the autobar, although he would have given years of his life right now for a quick double shot of guzzle. He emerged from a side door and strolled in the direction of his apartment. He couldn't make up his mind whether or not he had the time to spend five minutes gathering up . . .

No, he didn't. A helio-jet zoomed down before him and immediately in front of his building. Rosy Porras stepped hurriedly into a doorway.

It was Boleslaw and Kelly. They vaulted from the vehicle and hurried toward the apartment building door.

"That's that," Rosy growled. It wasn't as though it was disastrous. Rosy Porras had decided long ago in his career that times would come when a complete abandonment of all luggage and belongings would be necessary. To the extent that you could divorce yourself from such impediments, you were better off.

He had even left his transeiver in the apartment, on the off-chance that the computers might get a fix on him through that. But that was standard procedure on a job. Pop Rasch and Zogbaum would have done the same thing, of course.

He re-entered the hotel by the same door he had left only moments before and went to a phone booth and looked up the address coordinates of David Shriner and noted them down on the report he had surreptitiously taken from Martin Zogbaum.

There was nothing for it. Shriner's place was a good three miles away, but he'd have to walk it. He dare not use his Uni-Credit Card again.

It was approximately an hour later that he stood before the screen in Shriner's door. Rosy Porras snapped the fingers of his right hand in a fine case of jitters and muttered obscenities at the delay.

Dave Shriner's plump face lit up in the screen and he grinned. "Rosy!" he said. "Come on in."

The door opened and Rosy emerged into the foyer and then went on through into the ample living room. In a moment, Shriner appeared, yawning, from a bedroom. He wore a robe over pajamas. Dave Shriner was a second-string Tri-Di actor, noted for his comedy and exuberance.

He closed the bedroom door behind him and made a gesture with his head. "Ruth's asleep," he said. "Keep it low. I thought the deal was you were never to come here."

Rosy growled something and made his way over to the autobar where he dialed himself a double brandy.

Shriner said excitedly, "How did it go? Everything all set?"

Rosy took his drink back to a chair and slumped into it, suddenly very weary.

"Listen, Dave," he said, "a wheel came off. We're in the dill. You've got to help me."

The other's face froze. "What—what happened? Now, look here, Rosy. I didn't commit myself to doing more than . . ."

"Knock it," Rosy snapped. "Who'd you think you were playing with, some cloddy with a penny-ante racket? I've made arrangements to put plenty of credit to your account in the past and the things that you bought for me weren't as much as all that. You're in this now, if you want to be or not and the only way of helping yourself is helping me."

Dave Shriner, a short chubby man, good living oozing from his skin, went to the autobar and shakily dialed himself a twin of his visitor's drink. He turned back to Rosy Porras and said, "How did the romp pickle?"

Rosy ignored the word that irritated him and summed it up briefly. "We were halfway through the job when the police showed up. I got away, the others were probably caught."

"What are you going to do?" the actor said, trying to keep the tremor from his voice.

"I'm going on the run to South America," Rosy told him. "I want you to get on the screen right now and order me a shuttle rocket seat to Miami and from there a flight to Sãu Paulo. Then I want . . ."

Shriner laughed bitterly. "What am I going to do for pseudo-dollars? You know with . . . " he motioned toward the bedroom door ". . . I spend every bit of credit I get my hands on." He shrugged in deprecation. "That's why I lined up with you fellows in the first place and now look what you've done."

Rosy Porras brought the report sheet he had lifted from Zogbaum from his pocket and scowled down on it. He said, "You've been credited with nearly ten thousand pseudo-dollars. It's all been run into the credit records of this district. Zogbaum got that far before we were interrupted."

Shriner blanched. "Then I'm really in the soup."

Rosy waved the paper at him and growled, "No, you're not. I've got this. It's the only clue they might have had. We had this worked out foolproof. They'll never detect the difference, especially when they figure they've got the whole business in their hands."

"But they've got this man of yours who was doing the altering."

Rosy shook his head angrily. "That doesn't mean a thing. Martin Zogbaum had a list of some twenty names. He didn't have any call to be interested in individuals, he was just altering totals by code number. He doesn't know you from Adam and I've got the code sheet, the report sheet he was working from right here."

Dave Shriner finished his drink in a gulp. "And you think I'm safe?"

Rosy was lying, but Shriner was blinded by his need for hope.

"Sure, and the changes he made in the files were immediately effective. The pseudo-dollars are now in

127

your account. Get the Night Expediter on the screen and get to work. Get my tickets and then switch half of those credits to your account in Brazil."

"Half?" Shriner protested, regaining some courage. "Your cut was always one third which I paid over to you as supposed gifts or gambling winnings."

"That was before," Rosy growled. "Now I'm in the dill and need half."

Dave Shriner said, his eyes narrow with greed. "It wouldn't do you any good, Rosy. You can't spend my credits. I can buy those tickets for you but once you're in Brazil you'll be on your own."

"I'm taking your identification with me," Rosy told him flatly. "I've got some friends in Miami who can alter them enough for me to get by. They don't pay much attention in a foreign country anyway, just so the international credits are on tap."

The chubby actor was staring at him. "Are you drivel-happy? If you take my identification, what will I do?"

Rosy looked at him in disgust. "You'll go down to the Category Distribution offices tomorrow and tell them you lost them. Dream up some complicated story about falling out of your boat and having to strip out of your clothes so you could swim, or something. They'll issue you a new set. You're an actor, aren't you? With a well-known name like yours, nobody will think twice about it."

Shriner said unhappily, "Then what're you going to do in South America, Rosy?"

Rosy growled, "Keep in touch with some of the boys up here. When things cool, maybe I'll come back. Or maybe I'll just stay down there and make connections."

Shriner shook his head in sudden decision. "I won't do

it. I'd be sticking my neck out. Sooner or later, there'd be a check-back and I'd be in the dill and . . . ''

The heavy shooter was in Rosy's hand, held negligently, pointed at the floor between them. Rosy Porras's face was empty and cold, cold.

The chubby man stared in fascination at the weapon. He had never seen one, other than the props in the Tri-Di shows, before. And they, of course, were mock-ups.

Rosy said, ''Listen, get on that screen, you funker.''

Dave Shriner couldn't take his eyes from the shooter. ''Yeah, yeah, sure, Rosy. Don't get nervous, Rosy, you know me.''

Rosy grinned at him. ''I'm not nervous,'' he said. ''You're the one who ought to be nervous.''

Rosy Porras had an hour to kill before the shuttle rocket for Miami. He was safer here than any place else he could figure. So far as he knew, Tad Boleslaw and the police had no records of Dave Shriner, nor did either Pop Rasch or young Zogbaum know him. He was strictly one of Rosy's contacts.

Dave said worriedly, ''Won't they be looking for you at the shuttleports, Rosy?''

Rosy grinned again. The worst seemed to be behind. Most problems seemed to have been solved.

He said, ''That's one of the reasons I picked you, Dave. You're going to do a make-up job on me such as you've never done before. In fact, we'd better get going on that, eh?''

Dave Shriner brightened. At least it gave him something to do. He was beginning to get jittery sitting around with the gunman who no longer seemed to bear the old fascination, the old romantic air the portly Tri-Di had attributed to him. How had he ever gotten into this mess, anyhow? It was all Ruth's fault. Ruth with her extravagances, her constant demands.

Shriner went and got a make-up kit. For a moment, he stood back and studied Porras. The face of Rosy Porras was a natural for make-up disguise. And with the use of some of Dave Shriner's wardrobe, there was no reason to believe a job couldn't be done that would pass all except a really close scrutiny.

He started to work with care. There was ample time.

As he subtly changed the seeming width of eyes, Dave cleared his throat and said, "Rosy?"

"Yeah?"

"That shooter you carry. Have you ever—well, used it?"

Rosy Porras was inwardly amused. "Not yet," he said.

Shriner was silent for a long moment. Finally, "Rosy, what's the idea? The sort of, well, romps you do don't call for a gun. No crime today, that makes sense, calls for a shooter. It's mostly a matter of figuring out ways to beat the game. To scheme methods of cheating the banking section of the National Data Banks."

Rosy said gently, "To tell you the truth, Dave, it's a great comfort to me. A great comfort. And, how'd we know? Maybe a time'll come along when I do use it. You never know, Dave."

Dave Shriner cleared his throat again and began to add wrinkles to the other's forehead.

But his natural exuberance of spirit couldn't be completely suppressed. Finally, he said, "Rosy, what's the motivation? When you add it up at the end of the year, how many more pseudo-dollars do you actually wind up with than, say, I do?"

Rosy said, grumbling, "Probably none. Maybe I total less. Some years, when it's bad, I don't have much more than the dividends from my Basic Inalienable stocks. This year's pretty good, so far."

Shriner made a moue with his plump lips. "How can you say that? Here you are with the police after you."

"They haven't caught me yet," Rosy said, his voice grim. "And things won't be so bad in South America."

"But why? You're not unintelligent. You're not one of these cloddies who sits in front of his Tri-Di set all day, sucking on trank and watching the violence, drooling away. You could switch categories, somehow or other, get a job and a way of upping your living standards in a secure way. You must average a higher I.Q. than the usual cloddy who holds down a regular job and earns additional pseudo-dollars."

Rosy thought about the question.

"I don't like ruts," he growled finally, "and I don't like somebody telling me what I can do and what I can't. I don't like molds and sets of rules. I want my real share, what's coming to me, without a lot of crud thrown in." His voice had taken on a snarling quality.

"They think they've got it all worked out. Well, listen, there's never been a setup so smart that some stute can't beat the game. I'm doing it; I'm showing them."

Dave Shriner, his back turned as he fumbled with his jars of cosmetics, pursed his lips. This one was a real candidate for the Psychotherapy Institute. It was one thing, Shriner figured, trying to wrangle a few extra, unearned pseudo-dollars by this dodge or that. Quite a few people he knew at least tried it. But here! Rosy Porras was really far-out and this crisis was bringing out the worst in him.

Shriner went back to the job of disguising the other, silent now.

Rosy, after thinking it over, said, "Now what we've got to do, as soon as you finish, is go on down to the street and you get a cab and, using your credit card, dial me through to the shuttleport. I don't dare use your card until I get out of the country, and after having it altered by my Miami chum-pals."

"All right," Shriner said, in resignation.

Rosy Porras, a briefcase in hand, glasses on his nose, and a harried expression on his face, hustled across the shuttleport tarmac toward the waiting shuttle-rocket. He was a man in his mid-sixties, his hair heavily gray at the temples, his jowls heavy and loose with age.

He allowed a stewardess to take his arm at the top of the ladder and to help him to his seat. He breathed heavily as though the quick walk to the craft and then the climb up the ladder had winded him.

Rosy grinned inwardly. He was getting a kick out of putting this over. Dave Shriner, the actor, would have been proud of him had he been able to see the show.

He had lied to Dave. It was going to take that so-called Bunco Squad of Boleslaw's a few days to untangle all the changes Martin Zogbaum had made in the credit files, but it was only a matter of time till they traced them all down, now that they knew what they were looking for. They'd get to Dave Shriner's account last of all, perhaps, but they'd find that, too. Rosy's chance was to get to South America by tomorrow and find some way of converting those credits into something else, before the National Data Banks got around to canceling them. He had left betrayal of Pop Rasch, Martin Zogbaum and Dave Shriner behind him, but with the old Rosy Porras good fortune, he ought to be able to make it himself.

In his seat, he peered with supposedly aged eyes out the porthole. They would be taking off in minutes.

Tad Boleslaw sank into the seat next to him. "Hello, Rosy," he smiled. "Or would it be more appropriate to just call you Phidias? Things don't look so Rosy."

For a brief second Rosy gaped at him, then his hand flicked for his left shoulder and the harness there.

Boleslaw's left hand, in turn, chopped out, all but breaking the other's wrist.

The Bunco Squad patrolman said grimly, "That's the little item that busted your rosy luck, Porras. We didn't have the time to organize a really all-out man-hunt—they're not often called for these days. But we knew you'd probably try to get out of town, and probably be disguised. There was just one thing. We knew you liked to carry that shooter, Porras, just like the big, bad men of the old days. And all we had to do was spot metal detectors here and there in the appropriate places, such as shuttleports. Few men carry shooters anymore, Phidias, and yours showed up like a walrus in a goldfish bowl."

XIX

Tad Boleslaw was still in his bathrobe when his phone screen rang. He yawned and went over to it. He and Jim Kelly had been out into the wee hours the night before, on that Rosy Porras job and had planned to take the day off. In their new Bunco Squad, the decision when to work was in his hands. It had to be, since the job involved almost any hours.

He sat down at his desk and activated the screen.

It was Lieutenant Norm Schmidt and he was looking both puzzled and less than happy.

"Cheers, Norm, what spins?" Tad said. "I wasn't figuring on coming in today."

"Well, don't," Schmidt said glumly. "I won't mince around, Tad. You're indefinitely suspended."

"What!"

"That's the message. Came right down from the commissioner himself."

"But—but, *why?* You mean that he's not happy with the Bunco Squad thing?"

"I just don't know, Tad. I haven't the slightest idea. I don't know anything at all about this, Tad."

"Well," Tad said aghast, "what do you mean, indefinitely? I haven't been dismissed, have I? Don't I even go back to being an ordinary patrolman?"

The lieutenant sucked in air and shook his head. "That's all I know, Tad. You're indefinitely suspended from the Center City Police Force."

"Well, does my pay continue?"

The other shook his head as he said, "No. You're on your own."

"Holy jumping Zoroaster! But what did I do? Don't I get a hearing or anything?"

"No. No hearing. You're no longer on the force, as of now. Oh, just one other thing. You're to remain in your apartment until contacted."

"Contacted by whom?"

"I don't know. I guess that's all, Tad. Sorry as all hell." The face faded.

Tad stared at the blank screen, bewildered.

And it was then that the door buzzed.

He looked up at the identity screen.

A girl stood before it. A girl he had never seen before. He came to his feet and went over to open up for her.

Had he not been in such a mental turmoil, he would have considered the fact that he had never seen his caller before. She was a clever little trick, as he could see through the door. Her light brown hair was done in the latest ultra-short cut and there was a pertness to her face that gave a quick impression of youth. You looked twice before realizing that she must be nearly Tad's age.

Tad opened up and said, questionably, "Hello."

She said, "You're Tad Boleslaw?"

He nodded and said, "Come on in, Ms. What can I do for you? Frankly, I'm waiting for someone to contact me, and I don't know how much time I have."

She ignored that. "Probably nothing," she said.

"All right," he said amiably enough. "Have a chair. Drink?"

She took in his bathrobe and pajamas get-up.

He said, "I was up late last night. I don't want a drink

this early, this soon after getting out of bed. But if you do . . . ''

She occupied his comfort chair, holding her carry-all primly on her lap, and said, ''You might dial me a vodka martini.''

''No.''

She looked at him and blinked.

He walked over to his bar, and said, ''I have one of these damned automatic things, it came with the apartment, but the only time I use it is when I'm so short of credit that I can't afford decent guzzle. Other than for mixers and ice, that is.''

''You mean you mix your own drinks?''

''That's right. I hate gadgets. Something goes out of a mixed drink when they're all exactly alike, fraction of a gram by fraction of a gram. I like my drinks the way *I* like them, possibly a touch more of vermouth in a martini than the professional bartenders who devised the measurements of those that you get from an autobar. Possibly I like a jigger and a half of Scotch or Irish in my whiskey and sodas, instead of a jigger.''

He turned to begin building the cocktail for her.

She was slightly taken aback. ''You mean you keep your guzzle right here in your own mini-apartment, by the bottle?''

''That's right,'' he said, stirring.

''Mercy-meo, how weird can you get?''

He said wryly, ''Pretty weird if you work at it.'' He brought the drink back to her, then sat on the couch. He looked suggestively at his wrist chronometer.

When she had finished half of the drink, he said, ''I'm sorry, Ms. But I'm supposed to have somebody contact me somewhere along in here. I suspect it's important.''

"Yes, it is," she told him brightly. "I'm the contact. I probably have a job for you."

"A job? I'm a cop."

"You were a cop, you mean."

Tad thought about that. On the face of it, she was correct. "All right," he said. "What's the job?"

"I can't tell you. However, I assure you, the fee would probably be something like twenty-five shares of Variable Basic."

He did a silent whistle, then said, "Look, Ms.—Could I at least have your name?"

"Frommer. Nadine Frommer."

"Fine. But how can I work on a job for you if you can't tell me what it is? I think I ought to mention that I've been suspended from the police force. But then I guess you knew. You said I *was* a cop."

"Yes, I knew. We had you suspended."

Tad stared at her. "Who's we?"

"My boss and I."

"Who's your boss?"

"I won't tell you as yet. He'll explain."

"He's a big enough shot to get me tossed off the police force, eh? Wizard. Why was I suspended?"

She hesitated momentarily as though wondering if she should tell him that. But then she said, "Because we didn't want any records in the National Data Banks about you working on this—job. You're legally a private citizen now, and the police are no longer filing records about your activities." She stood. "Shall we go?"

"Fun and games," Tad growled, standing too. "Look, tell me this much. Should I carry a shooter?"

She looked at him questioningly.

"A gun, a gun. Is this the sort of a—job, on which I

should expect trouble to rear its ugly head? You mentioned twenty-five shares of Variable Basic. I assume I'm going to have to earn it the hard way.''

She bit her lower lip. ''Why—why, I suppose so. I—I don't know.''

''Okay. Wait'll I get showered and dressed. I'll be just a few minutes. Would you mind going out into the kitchenette?''

When she was gone, Tad went into the bathroom and had a quick shower and shave. He didn't know what in the hell was going on. However, if the commissioner himself had been the one to suspend him, for whatever reason, so he could take this job, it shouldn't be too far out—he hoped.

He went on back into his living room-cum-bedroom and dressed, in civilian clothes, of course. Then he opened a drawer and brought forth a .38 Recoilless and a shoulder harness and strapped it on under his left armpit and then tested the feel of it. He slipped a half dozen extra shells into a side pocket and then got into his coat.

He called, ''All right, Ms. Frommer.''

She re-entered the room from his kitchenette and he led the way to the door and the elevator. ''Basement levels to get a car?'' he said.

''Street. I'm parked up there.''

He looked at her, even as he ordered the elevator to street level. ''Parked?'' he said. ''You mean you've got an autocab just sitting there, running up a bill all this time?''

''Not exactly.''

The elevator had them at street level within moments. They emerged from the building and Nadine Frommer began to lead the way across the street toward the park.

His eyes widened to see the limousine hovercar parked there on the grass. "Is that *yours?*

"Of course."

"You can't leave a vehicle parked like that."

She chuckled her amusement at his lack of sophistication. "You can if you have a number one priority."

As they got nearer to the hovercar, he could see that the air-cushion vehicle wasn't a hired deal. It had been a long time since he had ridden in anything save an autocab, except for police patrol cars. In fact, he couldn't remember ever having seen just this model before. It was much larger than standard and considerably more swank.

"Pop in," she said. And went around to the other side and took the place behind the manual controls.

When he was beside her, she flicked the starter, dropped the lift lever and touched the accelerator with her sandal-shod foot.

"Where's the nearest entry, so we can go under?" she said.

"Straight ahead." He was still taking her in, unbelievingly. "There it is. Where are we going?"

"You'll see."

She pulled up to the entry to the ultra-expressway and skillfully came to a halt on a dispatcher. She reached over to the dashboard and dialed her destination. Then she relaxed and folded her hands in her lap when the auto-controls of the underground expressway took over. Within moments they were up to three hundred kilometers an hour.

She said to him, slight mockery in her voice, "Okay, you're a policeman, or were, with ambitions of becoming a detective, so we're told. What have you detected so far? Or, is the word, deduced?"

He looked over at her. "That this is a government vehicle."

"Bravo."

"And that since you're driving it, you're a government employee, and you don't dress or do yourself up too badly, either, so obviously your job is a good one. You mentioned your boss. I would guess that you're the secretary of a fairly high-ranking bureaucrat."

"Well," she said. "Not bad."

The speed of the buoyant began to fall off and shortly they entered a side branch of the road, went on a few kilometers and finally came to an entry where the limousine came to a halt on a dispatcher.

Nadine Frommer took over the manual controls again.

"What else?" she said.

"Whatever he wants to see me about is either personal . . ."

"You flunked there."

" . . . or very hush-hush, since he called in a now-private citizen, rather than depending upon local police or federal ones."

She brought the hovercar to a halt before the entry of a rearing-to-the-sky building and swung the door open. Tad Boleslaw joined her on the walk and accompanied her to the massive governmental building, which it obviously was.

At the door, one of two armed guards touched a finger to his cap and said, "Ms. Frommer."

She nodded impersonally and said, "This is the gentleman of whom you have been informed."

The guard looked at Tad Boleslaw.

Tad began to bring forth his identification, but Nadine said hurriedly, "That won't be necessary."

Tad put the Universal Credit Card and his police I.D. back in his pockets.

The guard made a motion with his head toward a small red light which was flickering.

"You're carrying a shooter," he said.

"It's licensed," Tad told him.

Nadine Frommer said impatiently, "I vouch for this gentleman. If you wish, check it out with Secretary MacDonald's office."

The guard said, "Very well, Ms. Frommer." He touched his cap again.

Tad followed the girl down a short corridor to a bank of elevators.

Inside, she said, "Top," into the elevator screen.

It said, "Yes, Ms. Frommer." And they started up.

Tad said, "Secretary MacDonald. That wouldn't mean . . ."

"Yes, it would. Secretary of Scientific Research Walter MacDonald."

Tad Boleslaw hissed a sighing whistle through his teeth.

The elevator smoothed to a stop and they issued forth into what were obviously the outer offices of a very major bureaucrat.

"This way," Nadine Frommer said. She led the way past various desks whose occupants didn't pause in their busy efforts even long enough to look up at the newcomers. There was an impressive efficiency here which was mildly surprising to Tad Boleslaw. Under the present socioeconomic system of People's Capitalism, government office workers weren't noted for aggressive efficiency.

An elegant door opened before them as soon as Nadine

Frommer's face could be distinguished in its screen. They entered, passed through what was obviously a reception room, with two girls at desks, busily occupied with voco-typers, screens and other equipment of the secretary. One looked up, nodded and said, "Ms. Frommer."

Nadine nodded in return and said, "Betty. Mr. Mac-Donald is expecting us."

"Yes, Ms. Frommer."

She led the way past the desks and to a still swankier door which also opened before them.

Inside, Tad Boleslaw came to a halt. From what had just preceded, he had expected quite the ultimate in offices. To the contrary, the interior of Walter MacDonald's office was on the austere side. Tad got the feeling that this head of scientific research in the United States of the Americas had worked his way up the hard way and on the path had become used to certain surroundings and conditioned to them. Had his rank been a bit less Olympian, he might have been branded a weird.

The man who sat at the desk was recognizable to Tad Boleslaw from various Tri-Di broadcasts. However, he seemed older than Tad had expected and right now looked as though he hadn't seen a bed the night before. There was even a bloodshot quality in his eyes and he needed a shave.

Nadine Frommer said, "Mr. Tad Boleslaw, sir."

MacDonald began to say something but Tad held up a hand. "Secretary MacDonald, before you speak, is it possible that this room is bugged?"

The other looked at him blankly. "Why, why I wouldn't think so."

Tad Boleslaw brought a seeming auto-stylo from an

inner pocket. He said, "just a moment," and began carrying the device about the office.

MacDonald said, "What in the name of Zoroaster is that?"

"A mop," Tad said. "It'll detect any bug based on electronics."

Finally satisfied, he turned back to the nation's secretary of scientific research and said apologetically, "Thus far, Ms. Frommer has been very secretive and I've assumed that this matter is confidential. Before you revealed anything at all, I thought we might as well check out whether or not anybody else was listening in."

Walter MacDonald was impressed. "Very efficient of you, Mr. Boleslaw." He was a well-built, crisp man in his early sixties and probably held his years very well save for this present obvious weariness.

He said, "Sit down, Mr. Boleslaw, and you, Nadine."

Tad found a place across from the desk and relaxed. It was MacDonald's top, let him start spinning it.

"We'll waste no time on preliminaries," the secretary said. "Mr. Boleslaw, what do you know about nuclear weapons?"

Tad shifted his shoulders. "Precious little."

"Tell me."

"Well, after a suggestion by Einstein, the United States built the first ones and used them against Japan. If I understand it correctly, the original atom bomb was a matter of uranium and plutonium splitting into lighter elements that together weigh less than the original atoms, the remainder of the mass appearing as energy. When the war ended, the Russians surprised everybody by exploding their first atomic bomb in 1949. Great Britain got into the act in 1952, I think it was, and then France, China and India got into the race. The H-bomb followed the A-bomb, starting about 1952. Even the Chinese had them by the late 1960s.''

Tad shrugged again. "I guess that's about all I know. In fact, I'm surprised I knew that much.''

Walter MacDonald nodded wearily. "Just a couple of things to add, in the way of background. The first atomic bomb cost literally billions to research and finally to build. It was wartime and expense meant nothing. The Soviets spent less since they were able to ferret out some of our secrets and avoid some of our mistakes. By the time the French built theirs, the costs had dropped precipitously, since there were few secrets left and shortcuts had been discovered. By the time the Chinese and later the Indians joined the club, the cost was a mere fraction. The point I'm making, of course, is that we have finally gotten to the point where the manufacturing of nuclear weapons is not truly expensive, especially if only one or two were required.''

Tad frowned and said, "Well, yes, but none are being manufactured today.''

"We hope,'' Nadine murmured.

Tad Boleslaw looked at her.

"Let me, Nadine,'' MacDonald said. He went back to Tad. "So far as we know, you are correct. The world, in growing horror at the prospect of more and more nations being armed with them, finally called a halt. Nuclear weapons were internationally outlawed. Those stockpiled were destroyed. Inspection was so organized that the half dozen powers which had developed the weapons could make no more. And the tiny nations could not afford the original research that would be needed.''

The science secretary hesitated before going on. ''But there is another aspect we should mention. Those first bombs weighed tons. But this is the age of miniaturization. Within a few years, we already had nuclear weapons so small that they could be fired by artillery. By the time the bombs were finally banned, they had got them down to the size of a football.''

''That small?'' Tad was surprised.

''Yes,'' MacDonald said and took up a small sheaf of papers from his desk and handed them to Tad Boleslaw. ''Please look at this.''

They were duplications of blueprints, formulas, math equations, and other scientific material. Tad looked through them, scowling. He looked up finally and shook his head. ''I'm a layman. I'm completely out of my depth.''

''Mr. Boleslaw, those are the complete plans enabling any even averagely competent physicist to construct a nuclear mini-bomb.''

Tad hissed a whistle through his teeth. ''I hope you don't just leave them sitting around.''

''Mr. Boleslaw, I have not seen these plans for years. You see, although the major powers no longer construct nuclear weapons, I am sure we all have the plans for them, and all other pertinent information, in our data banks. Such ultra-secret information, of course, calls for the highest priority, the very highest, before it can be tapped. Theoretically, it is impossible for an individual to gain access to this information.'' He came to a weary halt.

Tad said in puzzlement, ''What are you getting at?''

145

"Yesterday morning, when Ms. Frommer entered this office, preparatory to my own arrival, she found this complete set of blueprints and specifications sitting on my desk. As I say, I have not seen these plans for years."

Tad was staring at him. He said, in disbelief, "Where did they come from?"

Walter MacDonald took up another piece of paper and handed it over to the ex-patrolman.

"A letter," Tad murmured. "You seldom see a letter any more in this day of instant communication with anybody, anywhere, at practically no cost, through your transeiver."

The letter was on a ripple finish, twenty-four weight, fifty per cent rag-content white paper. There was a two word letterhead, very neatly printed in black. It read:

EXTORTION, INC.

Tad Boleslaw looked up at the scientist and then over at his secretary.

"Read it," MacDonald said, brushing his hand over his eyes in a gesture of tiredness.

EXTORTION, INC. is in possession of the plans for the economical manufacture of the nuclear mini-bomb. Unless its demands are met, copies of the said plans will be mailed to the governments of every nation on Earth, including Egypt and Israel, India and Pakistan, Cuba, and all African countries.

The demands are as follows:

1. Ten million pseudo-dollars to be deposited to our account in Switzerland.

2. Guarantee that no efforts to prosecute any member of EXTORTION, INC. will be taken.

3. The Intercontinental Bureau of Investigation,

*or any other police organization, will not be brought
into this matter. Failure to comply with this will
mean immediate doubling of the amount involved
to twenty million pseudo-dollars and continuation of
failure to comply will mean the immediate carrying
out of our threat.*

4. *Within the week, we expect you to appear on
national Tri-Di with a simple announcement of
your acceptance. We will then contact you further
with details of how to deposit the sum demanded to
our account.*

> *Sincerely,*
> *Executive Committee*
> *EXTORTION, INC.*

Tad Boleslaw reread it.

He ran a finger over the print of the letterhead. "Hand
set," he murmured, "and undoubtedly printed on an
old-fashioned platen press." He looked more closely at
the typing. "Hand typed on an old-fashioned electric
typewriter by an expert typist."

He looked up at Walter MacDonald, and said, "Why
me? Why didn't you immediately turn it over to the IBI?"

"How did it get on my desk?"

"I wouldn't know."

"It's practically impossible to get into this building, not
to speak of getting here into my office, unless you're a
government employee with correct identification. But,
above all, how did these members of Extortion, Incorporated ever get into the data banks to secure these plans?"

Tad looked at him, waiting for the science head to go
on.

MacDonald said, "There's only one possibility. These

extortionists have in their ranks some very highly placed employees of this department of government. If so, I have no reason to believe that they might not also have infiltrated the Intercontinental Bureau of Investigation, as well as the National Data Banks. In short, if I attempted to resort to the police, national or otherwise, the blackmailers might immediately know it and then the ten million pseudo-dollar demand would increase to twenty million.''

''So that's why you've called me in as a private citizen, which I now am.'' There was a trace of bitterness in Tad's voice.

''Yes. It was Ms. Frommer's suggestion and I'm grateful for it, even though it turns out to be a straw which I am grasping for. I got in touch with my very close friend, Commissioner Marvin Ruhling and he suggested you and suspended you from the police force, so that you could take the assignment. You will, of course, be amply rewarded. Frankly, I am completely out of my depth, Mr. Boleslaw. I know nothing about such matters as this. I need advice.''

Tad Boleslaw had put the extortion demand back down on the scientist's desk. Now he pointed to it and said, ''If you turned it over to the IBI boys they'd go to work with a team of hundreds of agents. There's a lot of things for them to work on. Who has access to the data banks? Who has access to this office? This paper? The type used, which is 18-point Stymie, a type face going back to the 1930s—I know because printing was a hobby of mine when I was a kid. The IBI might crack this in an hour or two.''

Nadine Frommer said, without inflection, ''And this executive committee of Extortion, Inc. might have those plans on their way to every two-by-four government on

148

the planet in ten minutes. Then the race would be on between such countries as Israel and Egypt to see who'd get theirs built and dispatched first.''

Tad looked at her thoughtfully, then back to Mac-Donald. He said, ''Have you considered giving in to them?''

''Yes, I've considered it,'' MacDonald said hopelessly. ''Taking the whole thing to the President and putting it in his lap, with the recommendation that we pay up. But there's one major difficulty.''

''What's that?''

''Ten million pseudo-dollars are approximately what it would cost any moderately competent physicist to construct one or two nuclear mini-bombs. If this Extortion, Incorporated group got their hands on that amount of money and actually built the bombs, can you imagine the blackmailing weapon they would then have?''

Tad hissed between his teeth.

Finally, he said, ''There's another angle. There's an old police adage that you never finish paying off a blackmailer. He keeps coming back for more. You have no guarantee that this outfit won't hit you over and over again for additional amounts. How long ago was it these plans went into the data banks?''

''Some five years ago.''

''And how many people are there with sufficient priority to take them out?''

''That's it,'' the science chief said. ''That's why I'm so bewildered. Nobody.''

Tad scowled lack of understanding at him.

MacDonald said, ''No one person. It would take an order from the President. And then I, with half a dozen

149

other, very high-ranking officials, would have to combine our priorities to extract this information.''

Tad took up the sheaf of plans again and stared at it. ''Old-fashioned Xerox duplication,'' he said.

He shook his head and looked at the Secretary of Scientific Research again. ''What did you expect me to do?''

''Why, I—I don't know. I've been grasping at straws, as I told you.''

Tad Boleslaw came to his feet. ''Well, there's nothing I can do. There's one thing I can add to that warning about blackmailers coming back over and over again.'' He pointed at the letter. ''They don't even offer to return the mini-bomb plans to you upon you paying off.''

Nadine Frommer said, in astonishment, ''You mean you refuse the job?''

''That's exactly what I mean,'' he told her.

''But—you haven't even asked what Mr. MacDonald would pay you for your assistance.''

MacDonald put in, urgently, ''It would not be dependent upon your success. You would be well-paid whether or not you succeeded.''

Tad said tightly, ''I'm an ex-cop, not a crook. Perhaps I'll be a cop again, shortly. When the suspension is raised. There's nothing I can do, and I don't take pay from people just because they're frightened and at their wits end, if I can't help them. The moment I started prowling around in your outer offices there, trying to check out who might have come in here and left the letter and the copy of the plans, then your Extortion, Inc. would be tipped off and you'd have the same situation as if you rang in the IBI. If you want police help in this, then don't rely on a single man in strange seas and out of his depth. Bring in your hordes of government police.''

"Then you definitely refuse to take the job?" Mac-Donald said.

"Yes."

The other's voice turned cold. "Then don't rely too much on that suspension being lifted. When I inform my friend, the police commissioner, that you refused to cooperate in this most pressing matter, I assume that he will take a dim view of it."

Down at the building entrance, Tad Boleslaw dialed an autocab and when it arrived, retraced the route over which Nadine Frommer had brought him.

He was disgusted. Far from getting anything out of this, he was being put to the expense of transporting himself back home. He supposed that he could have asked Mac-Donald for his expenses, but somehow he hadn't been able to bring himself to it, particularly in view of the other's anger there at the end.

He was unhappy, but he had no regrets. There was simply nothing that he, Tad Boleslaw, could possibly do that the IBI couldn't do better and, with all of their manpower, much more quickly.

He dismissed the vehicle at the street level entry to his building and took the elevator to the level of his mini-apartment. Still feeling disgruntled, he entered his living room and went immediately over to the bar.

He fished around and brought forth the bottle of Polish vodka and held it up to the light to check the contents. It was about half full. He poured himself a stiff slug into one of the glasses which sat above the bar top and knocked back about half of it.

"Now that's real guzzle," he muttered appreciatively. He sucked air in over his palate, the better to savor the flavor of the drink. He knew damn well that when his present supply of premium liquor was exhausted he wasn't going to be able to afford more. Not with his police pay no longer coming in.

He turned to walk over to his comfort chair and began to bring his glass up to his lips again. Felt the blackness rushing in. Tried to steady himself on the back of the chair. Crumbled to the floor, dropping the glass on the way down.

XX

When he awoke in the morning, his head was a burning agony and he stank of vodka. The carpeting in his vicinity was impregnated with the spilled guzzle and some of it had soaked into his clothes.

He sat up, groaning. He muttered, ''What in the name of the Holy jumping Zoroaster happened?''

He staggered erect and made his way into the kitchenette and to the sink there. He turned on the cold water and put his head under it. When he came erect, to fumble for a towel, he spotted something on the small table, something that didn't call for being there.

He went over and took it up, even before drying himself.

The letterhead read EXTORTION, INC.

> *Mr. Boleslaw:*
>
> *You have seen fit to disobey Demand Three. Your supposed suspension from the police was simply camouflage and we do not accept it.*
>
> *Please inform your employer, Secretary MacDonald, that the sum required by Extortion, Inc. will now be twenty million pseudo-dollars and that you will either remove yourself from this matter or our threat will immediately be implemented.*
>
> *Sincerely,*
> *Executive Committee*
> *Extortion, Inc.*

He shook his head in attempt to achieve clarity and stared at the note for long moments.

"You boys aren't as efficient as you'd like to put over," he muttered. "Somebody got the wrong message."

He wobbled back into the living room and over to his bar.

"Dammit, I hope the hell you didn't put mickies in every bottle in my stock."

But it wasn't that. Investigation indicated that, instead, every one of the glasses which lined the top of his bar had a minute amount of powder in it. Whoever had wanted to be sure that he took his knockout drops, had simply poisoned every glass available.

He sank down into a chair and ran his fingers through his wet hair. "But why?" he complained.

And came up with no answer.

Dammit, he had wanted to be a detective. All right, here was something to solve.

But there was no answer. And, for that matter, there was no answer to a lot of things about this whole ridiculous mess of an affair.

But there had to be. What was the old wheeze that Sherlock Holmes used to pull on Watson? Something about eliminate the impossible and what is left, no matter how seemingly improbable, is the actuality.

All right, wizard. MacDonald said that it was impossible for the data banks which contained the nuclear mini-bomb plans to have been tapped. It was also impossible for an outsider to have penetrated to the office of the Secretary of Scientific Research. It was also impossible that . . .

He came to a halt, intuition taking over.

After a few moments he rose to his feet and stripped

himself out of his drink-impregnated clothing. He went on into the bath and showered and shaved, went back into the living room-bedroom, got fresh clothes on and then sat down to his phone screen at the desk.

He said into the screen, "I want the offices of Secretary Walter MacDonald, of the Department of Scientific Research."

The face that filled the screen was new to him.

"Offices of Secretary MacDonald," she said briskly.

Tad said, "This is Boleslaw here. I'd like to talk to Ms. Frommer."

"Could you state your business, sir? Miss Frommer is always busy."

"She'll be busier still," he said bluntly. "Tell her that Tad Boleslaw has changed his mind and will be down as soon as an autocab will bring him."

He switched off the phone and grunted.

Nadine Frommer met him in the reception room outside Secretary MacDonald's office. Her eyes were wide. "Are you mad?" she said.

"If you mean crazy," he said grimly, "no. If you mean angry, yes. Come on, I want to see your boss." His characteristic easygoing air was gone like the snows of yesteryear.

"I'm not sure that it's a good idea," she said worriedly.

"Come on, come on," he growled. "Sooner or later, I'll see him. I've got something." He brought the letter he had found in his kitchenette from his pocket and waved it in her direction.

She shrugged light shoulders and approached the door to the private office of the chief of scientific research. It opened before them.

Walter MacDonald was as before, if anything, his exhaustion showing more definitely. Tad Boleslaw wondered if he had missed another night of sleep.

The scientist frowned at him. "What possibly could have happened to make you change your mind? On thinking it over, what you told me, your reasons for refusing the job, made sense. I wouldn't have gone through with my threat to try and blacklist you through the commissioner."

"Have you taken any steps as yet?" Tad demanded.

"No. No, I suppose I should," the other said in exhaustion. "But no matter what I do will be wrong."

Tad Boleslaw plunked himself down in the same chair he had occupied the day before and tossed the new letter to the desk before the scientist. MacDonald picked it up wonderingly.

Tad said, ignoring the stare of Nadine Frommer, "Yesterday, when I got home from here, I took a drink. I needed it. The glass had been loaded with knockout drops. When I awakened this morning, I found that on the table of my kitchenette."

MacDonald said, indicating the letter, "But this is ridiculous. You didn't accept the job."

Tad ignored him. He said, "The implication was that while I was here in your offices, somebody broke in and doped my glasses and then, last night, while I was under the influence of the drug, entered my apartment again and left this letter. But that's not what really happened. The letter was written and stashed on that table before I even met you, and before you gave me your pitch."

Nadine Frommer said, "What in the name of Zoroaster are you talking about?"

Tad pointed at the letter. "There's been a lot of misdirection and I'm a cloddy not to have caught on sooner.

However, answer me this. How many members are there in Extortion, Incorporated?"

MacDonald said, in puzzlement, "Why, how would I know? Evidently, quite a crew to accomplish all this."

"To accomplish all what? Why need there be more than one?"

Nadine blurted, "Why, that's ridiculous. The letters were both signed the Executive Committee."

"Wizard, that's the way they're signed, but so what? The way the letter is worded, and all, the implications are that a whole flock of bad-os are involved, but we've seen nothing that couldn't have been accomplished by one person. A real stute, admittedly, but one person. Somebody who could handle handset type, somebody who could set up a small platen press, somebody who could use an old fashioned electric typewriter and an old-type Xerox. Somebody who was cool enough to put knockout drops in an ex-cop's glasses on his bar, while he was in the bathroom taking a shower and planting a letter on the kitchenette table, knowing that he would leave the apartment before going in there."

Both of them were staring wide-eyed at him.

Tad said, "Who contacted Commissioner Ruhling and made the arrangements to suspend me so that I could take this job?"

MacDonald scowled. "I sent Nadine over. I was afraid a phone call might be tapped."

Tad said, "I'll tell you something about a man's Dossier Complete. There is one section devoted to his personal peculiarities, his little habits, idiosyncracies, vices, and so forth. One of mine is that I don't use my autobar, I spend a substantial amount of my income on real guzzle, and mix my drinks in my own apartment. It's off-beat, so undoubtedly it's in my dossier. People such as Lieutenant Schmidt, who have been in my place, and have had a drink there would know about it. And it would be his duty to report it, for listing in my dossier. Anybody who has a priority rating high enough to check a man's Dossier Complete could find out about it, and set me up to be doped the way I was. We'll have to find out why it was that the commissioner, who isn't too very smart, picked me for this job, rather than, say, some detective with more experience.''

They were still both staring at him as though he were drivel-happy.

He said, ''Another thing. You claimed that it was impossible for anybody to tap that information from the data banks. All right. How long has it been in the data banks?''

MacDonald said, ''Five years.''

''Wizard. Who could have Xeroxed those plans back *before* they were ever filed away in the National Data Banks?''

MacDonald's eyes turned to his secretary.

Tad snapped, ''I assume you have top priority so far as the data banks are concerned. I suggest you look up the Dossier Complete of our little girl here. Under education, under hobbies. I'll bet you pseudo-dollars to doughnuts that somewhere along the line she's studied handicrafts, hand-setting type and printing in particular.''

''Why, this is absolutely impossible,'' MacDonald snorted in disbelief.

''Wizard. Take your pick. There's only two persons that could have pulled this romp. You and Nadine Frommer. At your age, and in your position, I doubt if even twenty million pseudo-dollars stashed away in Switzerland would motivate you. But our girl, Nadine, has a good many years ahead of her. Even if it was discovered, later, after she had fled the country, that the whole romp was conceived and carried out by her, the United States of the Americas would never let it become public. National prestige couldn't stand the horselaugh that would go up around the world.''

Tad looked at her. ''She made just one big blockbuster of a mistake, in spite of five years of careful planning of every eventuality. She couldn't imagine anyone being less pseudo-dollar hungry than she is. She couldn't expect an unemployed ex-cop to turn down a job that would pay off what amounted to a small fortune in his eyes. So she wrote that letter she left on my kitchenette table, before I even talked to you.''

His eyes went back to MacDonald. ''Tear up those plans. I suspect they're the only copy she had. She didn't need any more. However, ring in your IBI boys and send them prying into every place she might have stashed her little hand-operated printing press, her stationery, and her electric typewriter. Maybe she's already destroyed them—but maybe not.''

Nadine Frommer let out an enraged squeal and darted for the door.

Her boss looked after her in shock.

He said, ''Nadine!''

XXI

It was two weeks later, and they were on a rather routine investigation. It was one of the blackmail romps that Warren Hammond, of the banking section of the National Data Banks, had told him about. Tad Boleslaw, of course, had been reinstated, congratulated all over the place by Commissioner Ruhling, and had, to his further satisfaction, twenty-five shares of Variable Basic to his account. This brought him up almost even with his sidekick, Jim Kelly, who had been saving all his adult life—which didn't make friend Jim one iota envious; in fact, he was jubilant.

Tad suspected that it wouldn't be long before he got his bounce up to the detective squad. Everything was going for him. He was young in the force, but he had a nice in. In actuality, that Extortion, Incorporated farce had been like a Christmas present.

Jim Kelly told him, idly, as they were heading for their destination—the suspect of the blackmailing romp —"You know, Buddy Brothers has done it again. Did you hear about it?"

Tad had had his mind on other things. He looked over at his partner, bemused, and said, "What in the hell are you talking about?"

Jim Kelly snorted amusement. "Buddy Brothers, you remember. He was jumped again. There were two of them this time. He chilled them both. I tell you, that character's a one man vigilante group. A couple more like him and there wouldn't be a juvenile delinquent left in town.''

The cold went through Tad Boleslaw. He ogled his partner. He said, ''You have to be drivel-happy. When? Why weren't we in on it?''

Jim said, ''Hell, Tad, we're no longer on that sort of detail. Besides, it didn't happen in our old patrol area. Just outside of it. We wouldn't've been called in anyway. Mike and Luke were first on the scene. Couple of wop kids. They must've thought a hurricane hit 'em. One had a gun and the other a knife.''

''That makes five,'' Tad muttered. ''How can a man in a well-policed, civilized town, have to kill five kids —were they kids?''

''Yeah, they were kids,'' Jim said. ''A couple more of these young punk funkers. One was about sixteen, one eighteen. Good riddance.''

Tad sucked in his breath and said, ''At the rate he's going, he'll have finished off every juvenile delinquent in town. That is, if they were juvenile delinquents.''

Jim Kelly looked at him from the side of his eyes, obviously irritated. He said harshly, ''What in the hell are you talking about? I told you, they were armed. And they tried to stick him up.''

Tad said emptily, ''The first two he killed had criminal records. The second two didn't.''

Jim was disgusted with him. He said, ''They were just beating the rap. They just hadn't taken a fall yet for any of their romps. These last two, they were both armed, weren't they?''

Tad didn't answer directly. He said, less than happily, ''I wonder how much of a crime dossier these two had.''

Jim didn't say anything to that, but concentrated on

landing the patrol helio-jet in front of the home of their suspect.

Tad Boleslaw stewed about it. When the patrol was over—the suspect had attempted to skip, and would be easily picked up when he attempted to use his Universal Credit Card—he decided to go and see Norm Schmidt, but the lieutenant was out on an attempted armed robbery investigation.

He went on home and to bed and stewed some more. After a couple of hours, he gave up and got up and went over to his desk and activated his screen. It took him some fifteen minutes to get the information he was seeking from the National Data Banks. Buddy Brothers had had his shoot-out with the original blacks about two years ago. He'd had his second attack, the one with the Puerto Rican kid, a year later. And the Mexican boy that Tad and Jim Kelly had been in on, came, roughly, six months after. This last shooting by Brothers came only two weeks later, give or take a day or two.

Tad leaned back in his chair, his face blank. He thought about it and finally growled aloud. "This whole damn thing is accelerating."

Then something else had come to him. The first was black, and the second was a Puerto Rican, the third a Mexican, and, now, the last two were Italians.

What had Brothers said, when Tad had given him his name? "Are you a foreigner?"

A foreigner, in the name of Zoroaster? Wasn't everybody in America a foreigner, except the Indians? For that matter, offhand he couldn't think of a country in the world where the present inhabitants hadn't displaced earlier peoples, usually by force. The Jews in Israel were foreigners twice over; originally they had conquered the

Philistines and this second time they had tossed out the Arabs.

He went back to bed and stewed some more. He got damn precious little sleep, if any. At best, he drowsed, pictures of Buddy Brothers gunning down swaths of kids in the streets of Center City coming to him.

When he finally surrendered and got up, he went, still in his pajama tops—he never wore the bottoms—for his desk screen, as he was. Then he thought better of it and went into his bath and used the depilatory on his face, and took a shower. He then dressed himself with care in his dress uniform, which was snazzy enough in appearance to suggest that he carried more rank than he really did.

He didn't take time for breakfast. Instead, he sat down before his screen and sought orally for the information he wanted, rather than dialing. He wound up with Colonel Mathers, of the local National Guard.

He identified himself and said, "Colonel Mathers, I'm checking up on some matters pertaining to Charles Brothers." He read off the identification number. It evidently wasn't necessary. The colonel knew who he was talking about.

Colonel Mathers was a soldier of the old school, looksomething like General John Pershing of World War I. He was tight of mouth, level of pale eyes, and wore his uniform as though he had never worn other clothing in his life—since infancy. He said, his voice expressionless, "What can I do for you?"

Tad took a breath and said, "Some years ago, Colonel, Mr. Brothers attempted to join the National Guard. With his background, his military record, wouldn't such a man usually be offered at least a lieutenant's commission?"

"Yes."

"But he was rejected. Not even accepted as an infantryman or non-com."

"Yes."

"But why?"

"That information is restricted."

"I am a Center City police officer, Colonel. Mr. Brothers is now under our jurisdiction."

"So you have already informed me," the Colonel said, still without expression. The screen blanked.

"Wow," Tad Boleslaw said in frustration. He slumped back in his chair. It came to him that he was continually slumping every time he came up against the Buddy Brothers matter.

He thought about it. And not very successfully. He had precious few possibilities, and no real leads.

Was there any use attempting to get in touch with the Octagon, in Greater Washington?

He doubted it.

And he began to have some other doubts. He suspected that if he prowled around much more that sooner or later somebody was going to land on him and shut him up. He could be shut up easily—if he didn't want to lose his job. And he didn't. Only a small percentage of the population had jobs these days, what with computerization and automation. Automation, hell, ultra-mation they were calling it these days. You simply didn't need *people* any more in the factories, the mines and so forth. Almost everybody lived on their Inalienable Basic. So far as Tadeusz Boleslaw was concerned, the hell with that.

In considering that attempts might be made to shut him up, for reasons unknown to him, he remembered all over again that within twenty-four hours, Tilly Brothers had known that he had been checking up on her father. How?

However, he was a cop and a dedicated cop, and he couldn't leave it alone.

It was late in the day by the standards of the average man, but early for him, and he hadn't even had breakfast. However, he got up and went over to his bar and got down his bottle of Polish Zubrowka vodka, telling himself all over again that the world might think that Russian vodka was the best, but any Pole knew better. This came with a sprig of herb in it which colored it slightly and gave a special flavor. Buffalo brand, it would be translated into English. Bison brand was more accurate and there was a bison on the label of the bottle.

He took it back with him to the desk screen, and stared down for a long time at the instrument without turning it on. Then he poured a quick drink and knocked it back chuck-a-luck and got to his dialing again.

From the National Data Banks he checked back on the military career of Charles Brothers, more thoroughly than he had the last time. His division, his regiment, finally down to his company and then squad.

He shuddered when he went over the record of Brothers' company. Over the four year period that Buddy Brothers had been with them, they had taken something like two hundred percent casualties. Two hundred percent! How had Brothers lived through four years with no more than three wounds, none of them bad enough to send him back to the States? At the end of the four years, there must not have been a dozen other men who had gone through the whole thing in the manner Buddy Brothers had done. Four years of taking casualties. A death here, a minor hit there, a wound the other place, an amputation perhaps, that took you out of combat for all time—and probably you blessed the fate that did it.

But two hundred percent casualties! There just shouldn't be any such thing in military statistics. That meant that simply nobody was left alive, twice over, for that four-year period of time. And over and over again the new replacement kids coming in to fill out the depleted ranks, most of them, green as they were, going down the first week or two. The veterans, such as Buddy Brothers, after a year or so in combat had at least some chance of surviving. At least they knew all of the ropes.

Two hundred percent casualties! In four years? They must have used that regiment as shock troops, expendables, expected to take high losses.

His efforts became routine now. And it took him a full two hours to find what he wanted, a veteran of Charles Brothers' own outfit who lived in Center City. Had he failed, he would have picked the nearest city and started off all over again. But he found what he was looking for. John Cardin, once a corporal in Brothers' company, and at the same time Brothers had served.

Tad noted down the man's address; it was out in the suburbs. He got his cap and left the mini-apartment, heading for the car pool down in the basements of the building. There, he rented a Volkshover.

The Cardin home, he found, was a single family house, middle class, very neat, with a few children's toys on the carefully trimmed lawn.

The identity screen on the door picked him up upon his approach up the walk and shortly the door opened and a middle-aged woman in an apron was there. She was a placid-looking type, fifteen or twenty pounds overweight, and obviously busy at her housework. And surprised to have a police officer confronting her. She had probably never had a police officer at her door before.

She said, "Good heavens, what is it? Nothing has happened to John—or Jimmy—"

He held up a hand and smiled reassuringly. Tad said, "Nothing has happened to anyone, Ms. Cardin. It is just that I have a few questions to ask your husband. Nothing important."

"What—what has he done?" she said in alarm.

He held his smile, still attempting to make it reassuring, as he answered her. "He hasn't done anything, Ms. Cardin. It's not about him. It's about somebody that he used to know, a long time ago."

She was obviously relieved, and said, "Oh, well, John isn't here now, but he should be getting home from work at any time."

Tad said, "Could I wait?"

"Why, certainly."

She led him to the small living room and saw him seated on a sofa.

She said, wiping her hands on the apron, "Could I get you a drink? John usually has a bottle of something or other in the kitchen cabinet."

Tad smiled and said, "Thank you, no. We're not supposed to drink in uniform."

"Coffee, perhaps?"

"No thanks. I'm fine."

She left him and he crossed his legs and waited for possibly fifteen minutes. He wished he had a magazine or something, but evidently the Cardins weren't reading folk. Her husband finally entered.

John Cardin was somewhere in his mid-fifties, about the same age as Charles Brothers, which fitted in with the fact that he had served in the Asian War. His build was good but his face was wrinkled beyond his years. It wasn't a happy face, there was a great deal of weariness, and perhaps a certain sadness. A plentitude of wrinkles otherwise, but no laugh wrinkles at the side of the eyes. He wore dirty coveralls, and Tad wondered what kind of work he did. There were few jobs that got you dirty any more; automation took care of the dirty jobs.

He was scowling and said in puzzlement, "You wanted to see me, officer? About what?"

Tad Boleslaw stood and held out his right hand for a shake, in the way of reassurance. He said, "I'm Patrolman Boleslaw, Mr. Cardin. I wanted to ask you some questions about Charles Brothers."

The other shook hands, still frowning. He thought about it, then shook his head. "Charles Brothers? Never heard of him."

"It was a long time ago," Tad told him. "During the war. Sergeant Charles Brothers. Possibly you knew him as Buddy Brothers. He was in your company, but not your squad."

"Oh, Buddy," the other nodded. "Sure, I knew Buddy Brothers. Sit down, officer. What ever happened to old Buddy Brothers?"

"He lives right here in Center City," Tad said, reseating himself.

"I'll be damned. I never knew that. But it's a big city and we live out here in the boondocks. What did you want to know about Buddy?" Tad's host seated himself as well and leaned forward in his chair, elbows on the arm rests. "I haven't seen him since the war."

Tad tread carefully now. He said, "As a matter of fact, it's about that trouble in the Asian War."

"Holy Zoroaster," he said in disgust, "are they raking that up again?"

168

"Well, in a way," Tad said carefully.

The other was more than unhappy. He said quietly, "If they're after him, they'd be after me, too."

Tad shook his head reassuringly, and said, "Don't worry about it, Mr. Cardin. After all, you were exonerated, weren't you?" He hoped the hell he was asking questions that wouldn't alarm the other and make him clam up.

"Yeah, sure, we all were. The whole thing was hushed up, but good. The orders came right from the top. I can't see why in the crud they're digging it up at this late date. It happened over twenty years ago."

Tad nodded and said, pulling his notebook from his pocket and bringing out a stylo, "Suppose you tell me about it, in your own words, briefly."

Cardin said, "Well, there's no reason why not. It's all in the records, though. Why do you need it?"

Tad Boleslaw twisted his mouth judiciously. "I'm afraid I can't tell you. Orders."

"Okay, then," the other said. "We were down in the Delta, see, and we'd been taking a lot of hits. One hell of a lot of casualties, and we were all uptight. We'd been in the lines for three weeks and that's too long and that Delta was no joke. Anyway, there was this town called Soc Trang. It was a little dump, couple of hundred people maybe. The lieutenant, he figured that was where some of the sniper fire was coming from. And so we went in. I don't know how it started. Something just kind of snapped and all of a sudden we were all shooting."

He paused and wiped his mouth with the back of his hand, obviously distressed at the memory. Undoubtedly, he had kept himself from thinking about it for some time.

"Go on," Tad said soothingly.

"Well, Buddy Brothers, he was kind of the ringleader, you might call it. He always was a feisty little bastard. We didn't find no snipers or even any military-age men at all. We rounded up the women and kids and put 'em all in the schoolhouse and locked the doors and then we rounded up the men—they were all old, and wasted them."

Tad looked up, trying to avoid gaping at Cardin. But supposedly he already knew about the incident. He said, "You shot them all?"

"Yeah. That's what I just told you." He moistened his lips. "We'd gone drivel-happy, see? We were all acting like crazies. I don't know who the hell it was got the idea of burning down the school. Maybe several of us at once."

"I see," Tad said. "I don't believe I've ever heard of Soc Trang."

"Nothing never came out. The army was having a lot of heat those days about several other—massacres, they called them. And there was one hell of a howl going up back in the States, with the newspapers and senators and all. So the brass didn't want any more to get out and so they put the lid on Soc Trang. The lieutenant, I forget his name, and Buddy Brothers and a couple of other guys they were considered the leaders-like and they were bounced out of the service with some kind of special discharge handed all the way down from the general."

"I see," Tad said. He returned the notebook to his pocket. "You think this might have had any long-term effect on Brothers?"

The other shrugged hugely. "Damned if I'd know. I never seen him again. But you see, he'd been in it for years. I only was in for about six months before I took a hit. He got to the point where he liked the killing, see. Buddy, he never took no prisoners. He shot 'em. Sometimes, even if you had a prisoner he'd take him off aways and waste him, too, even after the officers maybe had told you to pick up a few of them for questioning. He hated gooks and he called just about anybody a gook that wasn't what he was. He didn't even like the niggers that was in our own outfit and was always gettin' into hassles with them."

"I see," Tad said. He came to his feet and said, "Well, thank you very much, Mr. Cardin. You've been very cooperative. I hate to have brought all this up again for you—after all these years. I'm sure that we won't be bothering you further."

Cardin looked at him, sickness behind his eyes. "Nothing at all," he said.

"And please thank Ms. Cardin for me," Tad said, heading for the door.

XX

When Tad Boleslaw walked into the office of Norman Schmidt, the lieutenant looked up.

He said, "Cheers, Tad. What spins? What're you doing in uniform? I thought this was one of your days off. You like it so much, you just can't bear to take it off?"

Tad ignored the last, nodded greeting and sat down. "It's my day off, but there was something I wanted to check out. Norm, Charles Brothers is a psycho. He's as far around the corner as you can get."

"What in the hell are you talking about?" The older man reached for his stubby briar, scowling. He pulled his pound tin of pipe tobacco toward him, flicked off the lid and began to load up.

Tad said, "I've been talking to a war buddy of his. He said that Brothers saw so much action that he finally liked to kill. He'd shoot the prisoners and so forth. Then one day he led his men into one of those civilian massacre things. They killed a whole village of them, burning the kids up in the schoolhouse."

Lieutenant Schmidt flinched at that. He was a married man with several children of his own.

Tad held his peace for the time.

The older cop said finally, "That was a long time ago, Tad. More than twenty years. The median age in the United States of the Americas is twenty-five. In short, most people can't even remember back to the Asian War. A lot of us did things that we don't like to think about anymore. I was part of a bomber crew in the Asian War. Tail gunner. Zoroaster only knows where some of the bombs we dropped went. We even dropped bombs on towns that were supposedly in the part of the country we were trying to defend. Who knows how many children the bombs that left my plane hit?" He paused, and his face was empty, there was the same sickness that had been in the face of John Cardin. "Probably more than the number that died in that school."

Tad didn't say anything.

The older man spoke up again, finally. "It was a long time ago, Tad."

Tad still didn't say anything.

Schmidt had let his pipe go out. He relit it with a match from the old-fashioned box of kitchen matches he affected.

He said, "Tad, it was a long time ago. Like I told you, I checked out the Brothers Crime Dossier. He had nothing at all on him until just two years ago when he ran into that black funker. A bad boy, Tad."

Tad Boleslaw nodded. "Evidently, he was. And what you say is true. Brothers has nothing on his record since the war, until that. But there are some other angles."

"Such as?" The older man's voice was skeptical.

Tad brought his notebook from his pocket. He said, "I checked out his daughter, Tilly. Just on, sort of, instinct. Two months before he had his first shoot-out she was gang-raped by eight street bums. They were never caught. Tilly is, at least just slightly, a bit around the corner these days."

173

The lieutenant, who hadn't been able to get his pipe going again, fixed his eyes on his junior and said, "Okay. Go on."

Tad said doggedly, "Brothers had a nice home out of town aways. He moved into the slums where he lives now. He began to collect guns. He joined the CPA and the police pistol team. He tried to get into the National Guard which turned him down in view of his Asian War thing, I suppose. They keep it very hush-hush."

"Go on."

"He began to what amounted to prowling the streets —armed. By the way, I suspect that he wears bullet-proof clothing."

"Why do you suspect that?"

"It comes back to me. The way he looked that night when Jim Kelly and I picked him up. Sophisticated bullet-proof stuff. The kind the army has. It's not hard to come by, surplus army stores and so forth."

"Go on."

"He's out looking for trouble, Norm. He finds it. And he has no mercy. So okay, his liking for killing was submerged for twenty years. But then his girl was raped. He's prejudiced. All these supposed muggers and stick-up artists he's killed are either blacks, Latin Americans, or Italians. Holy Zoroaster, even when I gave him my Polish name the other night he tightened up. He's a psycho, Norm. Even his wife left him a couple of years ago; she must have been afraid."

"So what are you going to do about it?"

Tad squinted at him in surprise and said, "I brought it to you, Norm."

The lieutenant put his pipe down into a long overflowing ashtray. He said, "Forget about it, Tad. We've got nothing on the guy. As far as the military is concerned, his case is long-past buried. As far as his shooting up young punks who have jumped him, who are we to argue? Better him than some poor innocent citizen who can't defend himself. He defends himself with a vengeance."

Tad said stubbornly, "I think we ought to look further into it, Norm."

"Forget about it, Boleslaw. That's an order. I get the feeling that you're pushing a little bit more than is called for. When I read the Brothers dossiers I got the impression that even after all these years, the Octagon was putting a damper on anything about his case. You're just about to be promoted to detective sergeant. I wouldn't want to see you antagonize some big shot and get your ass fired right off the police force."

Tad flushed. He took a deep breath. "Yes, sir," he said, "I'd like to request a leave of absence."

"Oh, you would, eh?"

"Yes, sir."

"Wizard. You're eligible. In fact, I think you're due for a vacation shortly. You could take it now. Just one thing, Patrolman Boleslaw. On your vacation, you do not wear your uniform."

"No, sir."

"And turn in your gun for the period you are away, Patrolman Boleslaw."

XXIII

Tailing a man is an art, particularly at night in a city of practically deserted streets. However, Tad Boleslaw had taken a special course in it at the Intercontinental Bureau of Investigation school. The IBI was willing and even anxious to give ambitious local police officers as much training as they could assimilate.

Obviously, the subject must not even suspect that he is being tailed. He must not be even vaguely aware of your presence. You walk across the street from him, considerably behind. Sometimes, when on the same side of the street, you walk ahead of him. You never look into his face. If you make that mistake, he might remember it, if only subconsciously, and then be surprised, possibly several blocks later, to see that face again. Unless they have reason to suspect they are being followed, few persons consider it. It isn't part of the usual experience.

Tad had about come to the conclusion that Lieutenant Norm Schmidt had been right about the top authorities still continuing to keep a lid on the Charles Brothers scandal. It was the only way he could explain Tilly knowing about his investigations into the dossiers. Brothers must have been warned that someone was prying into his past, and passed the information on to his daughter, inadvertently or otherwise, and she had attempted to take what action she could. But Tad didn't give a damn what the military wanted. This was a Center City matter, and he was a Center City cop.

It went on for almost two weeks and then there was a seeming change in atmosphere. Tad Boleslaw got the impression that either Brothers had made him, or that the man had something out of the ordinary in mind.

He wasn't particularly afraid that the other would recognize him. The small man had seen him only in uniform some weeks ago and even then only twice and for short periods of time. Besides, Tad had worn a bit of a disguise, had darkened his complexion and put pads of cotton in his cheeks to change the contours of his face. He would have had to be quite close to his quarry to have been easily recognized.

But this night the other was from time to time looking over his shoulder, seemingly a fraction on the nervous side. Peering, occasionally, right or left.

Brothers customarily varied in the route he took walking home. It was about a two and a half mile hike and there were three different ways he covered it. Tad Boleslaw had already figured out the one he was taking this time, and remained ahead of his quarry and, at first, on the opposite side of the street, which was even more than usually deserted this night.

Tad got the feeling that this was it. And something, resembling ESP perhaps, told him that the crisis was just about to be reached. He crossed back to the other side of the street and entered a doorway, nonchalantly thumping a rolled newspaper against his leg. The door was seemingly that to his home; he had noted from the other side of the street that the doorway was open. A delapidated apartment house, typical of this slum neighborhood. He closed the door behind him, all but a crack, and waited.

He heard a voice, and could recognize it as that of Charles Brothers, say coldly, "Hold it, you funker!"

And another voice, indignantly, "What the hell's this? There's no use sticking me up. Do I look like some millionaire?"

And Brothers again. "You damned gook funker. What're you going on the streets this time of night?" His voice was going high and furious. "Looking for some poor girl to rape, some honest citizen to mug?"

"Who the hell are you, a cop?"

Tad Boleslaw flicked off the dim light which illuminated the hall behind him and opened the door slightly wider. The two were only a few yards down from him. He had hit it almost on the nailhead.

Brothers was standing there, ineffectual as usual in his appearance, but his gyro-jet rocket pistol in hand. The other was a youngster, Puerto Rican, Cuban or Mexican, by the looks of him in the night light.

"I'm asking the questions," Buddy Brothers said.

The young fellow was indignant. He said angrily, "I'm going home from work. I'm assistant janitor at . . ."

"You're a liar," the small man sneered.

And then came something Tad Boleslaw hadn't figured upon. Charles Brothers dipped a hand into a side pocket of his jacket and brought forth a second gun. He tossed it to the feet of the other.

He then brought forth from a pants pocket an emergency wrist alarm and flicked its activating stud. Almost immediately, sirens could be heard in the near distance.

His mask of hate all but broke up, and the gyro-jet pistol readied itself.

"That'll be all, Buddy!" Tad called, and stepped from his place of concealment. Originally, he had planned to tackle the smaller man. Or, at least, that's what he had told himself he planned. Schmidt, stripping him of both uniform and weapon, had left him up in the air. He knew he was being a damned fool trailing this killer without means of taking him.

Charles Brothers swirled, gawking behind the lenses of his spectacles.

Tad had already pulled the cotton from his cheeks. Now he took off his hat and let it drop to the street, so that Brothers could recognize him.

The young fellow had shrunk back against the wall, his eyes, too, gawking.

Tad Boleslaw looked at the killer. He said, "You cried wolf once too often."

"What are you talking about?" he snarled, his gun now directed at the patrolman.

"The old fairy story about the kid who was a shepherd. They told him if he ever saw a wolf to sound his horn and yell wolf and they'd come a-running. But he got bored and he used to do it just for the Dutch of it, because he wanted the excitement. He used to call wolf when there wasn't any wolf. He finally got it in the neck, though somewhat differently than the way you have."

Brothers was staring at him, breathing deeply. The siren swelled in the background.

Tad shook his head and said, "I hadn't figured it. That first shoot-out you had was legitimate. He really did try to jump you. But then that kill love came back to you and all these more recent shootings have been setups. You'd find some kid, alone on the streets at night, and toss an untraceable gun at his feet, activate your wrist emergency alarm, and then let him have it. The way you let those defenseless people have it in the Asian War. You're drivel-happy, Brothers, you're around the bend. Drop that gun.''

The other's eyes were darting every which way. He brought the super-lethal weapon up.

Tad said emptily, ''Charles Brothers, would you shoot an officer of the law, pursuing his duty? You too are supposedly an auxiliary officer of the law, serving our city.''

''They were all gooks,'' the other said shrilly. ''They're all the same. They're no good. All you can do is kill them when you find them on the streets, raping girls, sticking up honest . . . ''

Tad said, ''Drop the gun, Buddy Brothers.''

Instead, the small man, incongruous as a killer with his glasses and his ineffectual mustache, turned and darted for the corner.

He made it just in time to dash in front of the siren-screaming patrol car—supposedly coming to his rescue. He shrilled first despair and then agony.

Lieutenant Schmidt issued forth, looked down at the shattered body, then up at Tad Boleslaw.

Tad said, ''He was setting this kid up for another killing. He tossed one of those illegal, untraceable guns to the sidewalk in front of him. He was all ready to shoot when I got into the act.''

Schmidt looked down at the dead man for a long weary moment. He said finally, ''I suppose there's a moral here, somewhere. Wars aren't the best thing in the world to happen. And they don't end—the results of them—when the actual shooting stops.''

Tad said, his voice empty, "I'll take the job of going over and telling Tilly. She obviously knew that her father was a psycho, poor kid. That's why she was afraid. She knew that it was only a matter of time."

Mack Reynolds

Ursula K. Le Guin

10703	**City of Illusion**	$1.75
47803	**Left Hand of Darkness**	$1.95
66953	**Planet of Exile**	$1.25
73293	**Rocannon's World**	$1.50